LIGHT

HER

UP

C.B.

WIANT

LIGHT HER UP

C.B. WIANT

LIGHT HER UP

C. B. WIANT

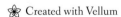

For anyone who believes bookmarks are for quitters. I believe in you.

Man is not what he thinks he is, he is what he hides.
— André Malraux

CONTENTS

WHEN AN EMPTY CUP OVERFLOWS

TIME FOR TEA

IT'S AN EARL GREY DAY. Students crisscross around me—the movement blends into an illusionary slipstream. The sound of shuffling books and the ruffling of pages merge into white noise. Slammed covers, pressed keys, skidding chairs and broken pencils are the ambient bass and percussion.

Everyone is fluid and working on a frequency that I can't reach. I can't connect.

I'm stuck.

Stationary in mental quicksand, I'm burrowing and surrounding myself in a claustrophobic torment of thoughts.

I have a tendency to be a little extra. As if too much sugar is added to my daily composition. My perspective remains milky and unclear regardless of any chemical additives. Muddled.

And the longer I sit at the University library, the more detailed my questions and anxieties become.

Can my own breath strangle me?

I know not thinking is just as easy as keeping my eyes open when I sneeze, or not sneezing when I stare at the sun.

Is it voluntary or involuntary?

How much actual control do I have over my life?

Am I even living?

I sit up straight in a standard, mass-produced, wooden chair —the same chair as everyone else. I'm grinding hard on my mental brakes to stop the cluster-fuck of my thoughts.

My fingernails drum against the cover of *MK Ultra Labs*. Bright red polish coats my right fingernails. Mauve polish slicks the fingernails of my left hand. *Rat, rat, rat,* I can imagine this noise is very annoying to those around me. Yet no one looks at me. And I don't stop.

Rain no longer races in stripes down the windows. Droplets stick to the glass like globules of fat.

A handful of brightly colored circles shake off the water before folding back into their closed umbrella forms.

Students funnel and pour out of doors from the surrounding buildings. They're mere ants scurrying for ample food for thought. They're so hungry to be the movement, a cog in the wheel. They are the future. Each of their steps has a purpose.

What am I doing?

Movement surrounds me, and I am still. My eyes track the motion.

If I don't move, is that considered a move?

Is inactivity a conscious decision?

Rat, rat, rat

THE SKY BRUISES from purple to black before I leave the *MK Ultra Labs* book unopened and discarded on the long wooden table.

Off the last step I hear, "Aviana."

Both of my feet lower to flat ground level, "Aviana, wait up."

I turn hoping recognition glints off someone's face, breaking the composure. A too bright smile flashes. I wave and the smile approaches.

"Hey, can we meet up?" Overtly smiles asks—then follows up with a request to catch-up—I'm assuming to re-up, I give my schedule at the bookstore.

I walk through unnecessarily heavy doors and into the night. Each heel to toe press is weighted as I drag myself down side-streets and sidewalks. I push my hands deeper into my pockets. The wind bites across my cheek. Brittle leaves and sticks shred under my sneakers.

A couple runs by me with their arms connected; they're holding each other close as they run side by side. I'm jealous of their warm link.

I slow my pace before crossing the Broad and Vine intersection and watch people scurry from exit to entrance. The warm meanderings of coffee dates and lunches on the patio have moved indoors for more intimate candlelit affairs.

There are no birds in the sky. The air is crisp without the sounds of insects. Maybe it's time for me to leave for a warmer climate.

It would be nicer if I could go back in time.

But how far back would I go?

When did this all begin?

It feels near impossible to reconstruct the past few days in a linear sequence. Fragments of suspicious activities, terrifying images, and misconstrued phrases overlap and invert themselves out of order. Only physical memories are clear. The rest is conjecture.

A car honks and I jump to action and complete crossing the street like a good pedestrian. I put my hand up in the universal sign for *I'm sorry I wasn't paying attention.* The driver waves back like he doesn't give a shit. He just wants me to move. I'm standing in his way and he's trying to make it to the football game. *What the fuck is wrong with me?* The game's about to start.

My feet continue down a path like a well-trained horse on a

trail to Woodcrest Apartments. I've been visiting on the regular. As of late, I might as well be paying rent.

Today I don't knock and let myself in through the faded pale blue door of apartment 936. The nine's upmost screw is extricated and rebelliously sways as a six.

The individual I seek is Ramona, an honor student majoring in Psychology. She sits in her white pleather armchair licking and sealing a blueberry flavored blunt. Her soft pink hair is in a messy bun and she wears deep red cat-like glasses. Periodically she changes the frames to coordinate with her hair color. For the past week, she exuded a demure 1940s pin-up librarian vibe.

I can rally behind any vintage beauty. I fully support confident women, especially those that get me high and make me think of what they'd look like naked on a B-52.

I jump the back of the red velvet couch into what I dub as my *brain chair*. Ramona sparks the blunt and passes it to me. Judge Judy enforces a zero-tolerance policy on the television in the background. I smile because I love Judge Judy. Truly, soul-deep, I love Judge Judy.

Ramona rearranges two leopards-print pillows beside her until she finds a notebook. The yellow cover has a large **A** written across its shiny surface in bold black marker. She drops the notebook onto her lap and looks up at me real expectantly.

A beat passes before either of us does anything, then she turns the volume down on the television. Which forces Judge Judy to use her inside voice. I'm passive-aggressively requested to use my actual voice. I take a deep hit to my lungs, and as I exhale I feel the sharp edges of my thoughts fade and smudge out, brightness and intensity dim. I take myself down a notch. Level myself out and couch-lock myself.

I CAN DO THIS.

. . .

I BLINK and try to focus on this moment.

Right now.

Across from me, I watch my friend fidget with her pen. She's an addict for my words, but they're vile and poisonous when they leave my tongue—like I'm spreading lies when I know I'm not. Words are about perception, and I fear she already has me boxed in. I'm guilty until proven innocent.

Our simple, mundane friendship has morphed. I wish times were different. Now, I'm her favorite mixed cocktail of convoluted insecurities and indecisions. All she has to do is sit back and sip my awkward glances and murmurs while I watch her eyes glaze over in a euphoric: *I can't wait to fix you, but I love watching you break more* expression.

I TAKE another hit and think strongly about bailing.

FUCK IT, I'm already here.

I SET the blunt on the ashtray and start a slow drip of words. "I've spent the last few hours rehashing what happened."

I unconsciously cross my arms, a subliminal attempt to protect my heart. It's an obvious tell. I uncross my arms. My right leg slips up and over my left knee. I uncross my legs and lace my fingers together on my lap. I uncross my fingers and have no idea what to do with my hands. I never know what to do with my hands. *How can such vital appendages be so traitorously awkward and twitchy?* I sit on them. Fuck appendages, fuck all of them; legs, arms, hands, vestigial structures, and ghost limbs too.

Ramona's head tilts to the side like my forehead is a two-way mirror into my mind and she reads me. I'm that transparent.

"Aviana, I thought you were going to study?" The gavel taps in the background and Judge Judy whispers a demand to order. The sound reminds me of the rogue six on the front door.

"I couldn't concentrate on anything but...what I did..." I mumble. I hate it when I mumble.

"You mean what you and Genevieve did?"

I cringe at the mention of Genevieve. Her name is a punch straight to the gut—my shoulders round inwards, my body curls to protect vital organs. "No, I didn't do anything with Genevieve. I was just the designated driver. She was already there with Hudson."

There's a pregnant pause before I ask, "How is she?"

"Doing as well as she can be considering the circumstance. Have you seen her?"

I jerk my head no. I haven't seen her or contacted her since *that night.*

Ramona redirects, "Tell me about Hudson."

I lower my head for a moment. All I want right now is to run out the front door. I want to hear the smack of the swaying six against the wood as my departing note. Being accountable is taxing. The gavel taps again in the background, mocking me. I smile because it's Judge Judy.

Logically, I understand running away defeats the purpose of arriving to start. But there's little logic to fear and its cohort anxiety—those two are overwhelming and suffocating, whether simultaneously or tag-teaming, they will always have my number and will never have my back.

I've been silent too long because Ramona follows her request with another. "You believe Genevieve, don't you?"

Don't I? Is no an option?

I nod, and with a boost of adrenaline, I get up to search the kitchen for a snack. I'm not particularly hungry, but the next questions are standard and I don't want to talk about Hudson. Even though I visit Ramona to talk about Hudson. It's a conundrum that has the tail leading the dog.

There are twenty-six cabinet doors and I open all of them. Tupperware stacks in the corner shelves. Mugs, cups, tea, and coffee accessories are above the coffeemaker. The heavies, such as pots and pans, are on the lower shelves. Spices are next to the stove. The illicit junk-food cabinet is the furthest one away. Everything is organized the same as it was yesterday. An irrational fear that one day, I'll open all the cabinets to find everything switched around makes me twitch. I head for the Oreo cookies and eat a couple.

Fight or flight—and I chose flight. Always flight. My emotions are in too much flux to remember the steps to calm myself down. It isn't D.A.R.E., F.A.S.T. is for strokes. Is it S.T.O.P? I'm feeling shortness of breath, a tightness in my chest. I'm feeling weak, *am I having a heart attack?*

I just want to be normal for a bit.

I place my hand on the refrigerator and give my weight to it. My forehead taps against the cooler surface. I take a deep breath... In and out, in and out. It's that simple. There is no need to complicate. I am the only complication. I need to get a handle on myself and eat another cookie.

Ramona hollers from the living room, "Aviana, come back. We don't have to talk about Hudson." I return with my metaphorical tail between my legs. I leave all the cabinet doors open. I'm tired of doors and their imposed boundaries. Black Oreo dusts the floor in my wake.

"Let's backtrack, last Sunday you left town. Where did you go?"

"Where did I go?" I parrot as I sit back down. The next question will undoubtedly be about what I did. Voices will rise during the hows and whys. I've heard this conversation before. I have the same conversation multiple times a day with myself. In my head. Or in my car out loud. Sometimes down the aisles of the grocery store. *Are these the early stages of schizophrenia?* I'm positive it's entirely normal to talk to yourself in the grocery store and to perform ballads in the car and shower.

I close my eyes, take another breath, and snatch the blunt. I make eye contact with Ramona and take a long drag. Smoke escapes my nose and I feel like a dragon.

I become aware of a slight glaze that glasses Ramona's eyes—which most likely mirror my own. Then like a snap or spark, I remember: A.W.A.R.E. Accept the anxiety, Watch the anxiety, Act normally, Repeat, and Expect the best.

"I went to a cabin in the middle of the woods," I say and press my free hand to my temple. The dull pain that has taken up residence behind my eyes throbs whole-heartedly.

I remember serving my self-imposed penance. Each time I got frustrated, I increased the luxury of the sexual favors I wanted to request for being the designated driver. I wasn't prepared to handle what I saw when I rolled up on Genevieve.

Ramona's pen twirls restlessly between her fingers. She's waiting on me to expound upon my comment. Her pen's drying out. I'm taking too long.

But I can't help but wonder if she feels a high off of my vulnerabilities. Or if me seeking her confidence gives her more of a warm body buzz. She is definitely getting off in some form, even if only subtly—she's glowing. I'm saying exactly what she wants me to say, and I'm not sure if that is a good thing.

I take another hit and release a sigh laced with smoke tendrils. I return the blunt to its maker and ask, "Remember Halloween at Ben's house?"

"You mean at Ben and Hudson's house?"

"It's always been Ben's house, Hudson just lived there."

"I remember going with you." A single eyebrow raises on Ramona's heart-shaped face; she turns her introspective gaze back to me. She puts pen to paper, "Tell me what you remember."

2

CRIMINALS RETURN TO THE SCENE OF THE CRIME

On Saturday, October 29, 2011, I wore leather shorts with knee-high boots that made me think foot amputations were a pleasant idea. With a whip in my hand and a top hat on my head, I was a demonic circus master. Hudson was less creative with just jeans and his zip-up hood raised. If anyone asked him what he was, he'd say he was the roommate, or a pedestrian, a student, or a jaywalker. Once he said he was a crowd surfer. Each option was equally lame. It made little sense to me, but I was drunk so everything was *all right*—not quite Matthew McConaughey *alright, alright, alright.*

"Remember when Hudson and I ran into you in the kitchen? We were getting refills on jungle juice, and before Hudson could take his first sip, there was a loud bang. Something crashed, or someone fell into... it was loud and possibly painful. Hudson gave me his cup and left to investigate the noise. Ben and Terra came into the kitchen a few minutes after Hudson left." I lean forward with both fingers pressed to my temples; my elbows dig into my knees. *Fucking Terra.*

Ramona swings her leg over the side of the chair. It dangles over the arm like a dying minnow on a lure kicking to life every few seconds. "Right, Tarzan and the fresh-faced white bunny." Ramona weaves her pen between her fingers and idles down memory lane with me.

"I remember the bunny looking at you like you were behind the barrel of a shotgun and she was in season." Ramona taps the pen on her lower lip as if debating to take the road less traveled. "And how do we *know* Terra?"

I appear normal. I reassure myself mentally, I am acting normally. "She's Hudson's past. At the party, I saw Ben later in the night sans bunny foo-foo. I'm assuming at some point she ran into Hudson." I stand and pace the room. "She was everything to him."

Suddenly I stop and stare up at the ceiling, "I'm a horrible person, aren't I? I should ask Ben for Terra's number, maybe I should call her?" I shake my head denying my thoughts, then laugh softly to myself. "That would be such an awkward conversation. What would I say? *Sorry for killing Hudson? I hope you guys had all the catching up you needed to at the party. He loved you long time.*"

Ramona shoots forward as if springing from a trap. "What do you mean you killed Hudson?"

"The cabin burned to the ground," I say under a whispered breath as I slam the door. The bronze six slaps against the pale blue paint. The sound doesn't satisfy me as much as I thought it would. I wanted a BANG. An announcement. What I received was excusatory, *pardon me thump.* good riddance.

I CAN'T steady my heart's pace as I knock on Ben's door. I don't even try. The thrumming of my heart matches my knocks. I buzz like a hummingbird, two-hundred and fifty breaths per minute.

Ben answers with a sandwich in his hand that promptly falls to the floor once he recognizes me at his stoop. It's been a second since he's seen my face and hyperventilating isn't my best look. Word vomit erupts off my tongue. "I can't go home. Ramona is in my head. I don't want to go back there. And I don't know where else to go. Can I stay the night? I just need somewhere to stay. Maybe a couple of nights?" My words and thoughts are on an endless loop. I begin again, "I can't go home..."

Ben's shock has his mouth dropping at the same rate as the sandwich. He quickly recovers and gestures for me to come inside. I scurry under his arm with my bookbag straps tight in my fists. I ramble a bit more in gratitude as we walk into the kitchen. I'm spilling words like an overflowing sink. I don't think either of us is listening to me. For all I know, I may be talking about leprechauns and Welsh kings. Either way, Ben seems to buy stock in what I'm selling and offers me a place to relocate temporarily.

In the kitchen, I walk straight to grab a mug from the charcoal gray cabinets. The mug advertises a golf outing win. After adding water, I carry the trophy to the microwave where I punch in the numerical code to create hot water for tea. Ben begins construction on another sandwich. Once the microwave beeps, I take my hot beverage and myself to the counter. I jump up on the stool and ask, "Can I ask you something?" My conversational skills are on par today.

I stare at the walls, if only they could speak, the stories they would tell. Any of the kitchen or hallway walls would know the answers; the flat surfaces are peaceful, welcoming, always the recipient. I'd rather talk to a wall than people. On most days, I might as well be talking to a wall. Or I am the wall and words just hit me without me absorbing any of the information. It's a toss-up.

"Shoot," Ben says as he sorts through the refrigerator shelves for cheese.

"Did Terra ever run into Hudson at the Halloween party? I didn't see either of them the rest of the night." I redirect my stare down at the tea leaves, wishing I were more psychic, less psycho. The bag bobs, a buoy of indecision. "Hudson never called me that night. The last time I saw him was... well I didn't talk to him before... never mind." Real articulate. My eyes move left to track Ben. He's finishing drizzling a line of ketchup. Red melds into the white of the mayonnaise. Both bread-ends connect and Ben takes a large bite of his sandwich. He looks at me as he chews and leans back against the counter with ankles crossed. He digests his thoughts. The ketchup and mayonnaise bottle lids remain gaping open, unsnapped, their condiments exposed.

"Listen Aviana, I'm sorry I can't tell you what happened. They left together in the early morning and he said nothing to me when he came back in the afternoon."

Ben takes another bite, and from behind his hand and with a mouthful he says, "But that's not unusual."

I nod my head, say goodnight, and take my bookbag and tea up the stairs and down the hall. The lights aren't on. My hands stick to the heat of my mug and don't search the walls for switches. I'm made of glass, always moving fast and crashing into broken shards. Now I make a concerted effort to slow down. I move like the walking dead I feel myself to be. I walk until I reach a dead-end and then open it. Darkness swallows the room. I chug the rest of my tea, bite back the burn, and set the mug by the door. I find the bed by touch and crawl against its surface until my face finds a pillow. I toss my bookbag to the floor with a heavy thud.

I try to stop being. And it works for a few hours.

WHEN I WAKE UP, it's due to light that's bright enough to burn my retinas. I scrunch back and turn my face into the pillow and towards the wall for refuge. As I open my eyes for the second time, I do so cautiously and come face-to-face with my face. My world abruptly slows down and focuses as if the sheriff's lights are behind me. Sweat prickles out of my pits.

A lined sheet of notebook paper has my face and naked shoulder sketched across its surface. There are light fingerprint smudges, casual caresses along the outlines and shadows. I study my image as my eyes adjust to the day's setting.

I must be in Hudson's room.

The realization is a bucket of ice-cold water. I shoot out of bed drenched in memories. I've seen glimpses of Hudson's sketches from behind his shoulder before, but never up close. Never like this. Never of my face.

Spinning, I survey the room and there is nothing of note. The only note is taped to the wall with a rendering of my face. The remainder of the room is a blank slate.

I have never been to Hudson's room, and I never found it strange until now.

Of course, I open drawers and search under the bed. His possessions are limited and ordered. His pens are buddied up against pencils. Folded shirts are beneath the sock drawer. The sock drawer only contains socks. The drawer with his boxer briefs holds no surprises.

In the closet, I find a black chest. I drag the chest to the center of the room. Objects shift in the ensuing move and I circle the chest like it's a living, breathing, animal. I evaluate its worn and dented form, debating my next calculated move.

I feel like Pandora.

The moment is heavy—the seal of the chest is the starting line.

Am I ready?

—On my mark.

Wait.

Taking a step back, I try to rationalize why the chest is still here. Either the police have a stockpile of evidence they're keeping a secret, or Hudson doesn't have many possessions. And if he doesn't have many possessions besides this chest, why is it still here? It must not have much relevance to Hudson's character or disappearance. The police have gone through his belongings and deemed the chest immaterial.

I cock my head to the side and squat down to level myself with the chest. Eyes to the keyhole, my palms sweat. It's strange fearing an inanimate object. I'm powerless to my rapidly beating heart. *Why isn't this chest locked?*

What I understand for sure is that this chest holds weight, and the curiosity is bound to kill me.

I lift the lid and instantly recognize the black leather backings. Dozens of black leather sketchbooks are within the chest.

I thought Hudson had only one sketchbook. I didn't think he had many of the same kind. He guarded his sketchbook like his *precious*. We've spent hours together pouring over pages, him drawing and me reading. Our time spent together was in silent awareness of the other. More often than not, I've been jealous of the tender attentiveness the leather binding received. Before Hudson would put pen to paper, his expression would soften and become reverent and honest. Each image is a confession. Each page feels a caress between his finger and thumb. *This is Hudson.*

How could they leave the chest as immaterial? Maybe these aren't all the sketchbooks. These may be the few of many. I have no idea of the original count.

My breath catches when my answer becomes boldly apparent. The sketchbooks are littered with images of me; my body parts, poses, facial expressions, or just my eyes. Rushed, harsh cross-hatchings. Some soft with stroked layering. Only a handful of the sketches are with my exact likeness. Most of the sketchbooks contain ideas and options of me. It's like he didn't know me yet, but he missed me. There's a sense of longing. A need for discovery. He was trying to find a perspective of me that fit. Yet instead, he found me. *The real me.*

The feeling of being analyzed like prey creeps against the back of my neck like an armored tick packed full of disease. An instinctive warning sends off an alarm.

I turn the page to see a woman's phone number. 'Emma,' with hearts next to her name. The hearts look more like peaches and butts than an actual heart. Too much rounding, not enough point.

I toss the sketchbooks back into the chest and slam the chest back into the closet. The hearts bother me in a way they shouldn't. Yet the brazen hearts aren't the root of my distress. They're just bad form. My concern rests in the stockpile of my likeness.

I rub my hands across my face and neck to suppress the crawling sensations—like I'm having a revisit from a bad acid trip. The prickly steps are everywhere on my skin. My feelings tangle, layer, and become too complex, too convoluted. My hands circle my neck, then rub up and down my arms. The sensation doesn't dissipate. I run from the scene and race down the stairs.

On my spin around the balustrade, I see Ben. His eyes widen when he sees me. I stop at the last step like I've run into an invisible wall—as if my negativity ran into his negativity and our magnetic poles repelled. We stare. *Am I trespassing? Did he forget I was here?*

Ben looks into the kitchen, back at me, back into the kitchen. He holds up a finger to tell the refrigerator he will be right back in a second and not to go anywhere. Then he grabs my elbow and pulls me into the office. "What did I do?" I ask.

He shuts the door. The room is all wood panels and smells like lemons. It's too clean. No one actually works here. They only call the room an office because it holds the desktop computer and a swivel chair.

Ben turns to me. "Terra is here." There isn't any humor in his voice like there was in mine. It's unfortunate that he kept the mood astringent like the room.

Well shit, I think as I take my seat behind the desk. The chair rolls back, and I hit the wall. I should thank him for the heads up. I should have a lot of reactions. But none come to me. I'm numb and on overload. My mind takes me out of participation, plucks me off the merry-go-round, and benches me.

The remaining conversation is an out-of-body experience. Our words are muted.

Ben leads the ghost of me back into the hallway to the kitchen where awkward re-introductions are re-made. Another husk version of myself shakes Terra's hand. I make animated awkward hand gestures and sit down hoping luck has its charms. The future is milky and my cereal is soggy. This is not natural. I'm not acting naturally.

Before I came barreling down the stairs, Ben and Terra were discussing recent events like news anchors. Terra flew back to be more available in case they find Hudson. Apparently, the past week has been the hardest week of her life. Frantic with worry, she installs herself in Hudson's case like she's always been here—even though she's only been here an hour. Either way, she's covering this story. She's the lead.

This is the second time I've seen her face, and it's two too many. I thought I had words to say to her. Yet, it's funny how reality is different—how it bitch slaps you with emotions and ties my tongue in a knot.

Ben briefs Terra on the most current affairs. We're all sitting at the kitchen counter, Ben in the middle. Their breakfast bowls are empty. Mine is full and continues to become mushier by the second.

The truth is in the pit of my stomach and it's tossing boulders all over my glasshouse. Inevitability hits me—I will shatter and bleed out everywhere.

"Did anyone see Hudson leave the cabin?" Terra asks. I shake my head in truth. Hudson was within the cabin as it caught flame. I'm not sure if anyone recognizes my head motion, or even if I'm considered a part of the conversation. No one tosses his or her eyes back to me. I'm just a spectator watching the live morning show. The co-anchors sip coffee and angle towards each other. I am the weird fan through the glass window without a poster proclaiming a shout-out request. I need a sign.

"There is no evidence of anything. But Hudson must have found a way to escape the fire. There is no record of him at any hospital. He's on the run. We just need to find him," Ben says with less hope than when he started his speech. The problem is that he doesn't believe his monologue. Still, he pushes the message. "We can search the woods around the cabin, see if there are any signs of Hudson," he continues. Hope is alive.

I nod. We are going fishing in an over-fished pond. The police have scoured the grounds and found no signs of life, but I don't want to be alone and left to my own devices. I follow my peers and the pressure builds.

———

THE ADVENTURE BEGINS and thankfully I pull shotgun in Ben's truck. I am tucked in as close as I can be to the window. No bandits or pirates in sight, only the birds flying.

Terra has enough room in the middle of the cab to sit cross-legged and fiddle with the radio. Anytime a commercial airs she changes the station. She spins the dial like it's a massive wheel on a game show and hopefully, she'll land on a prize. I hope for bankrupt or lose a turn.

"*Come to Rob....*" Spin. "*Discount SUVs...*" Spin. "*The ultimate...*" Spin. "*This week only...*" Spin to static, static, more static, then Taylor Swift.

I wish I had a legitimate shotgun. Instead, I settle for my little wooden dugout and pack up a one-hitter. The window creaks and groans when I crank it open to allow a courtesy smoke escape. I turn fully to the window and in a snap my one-hitter is cherry red and smoke is rooting in my lungs. My exhale goes off into the wind. Terra coughs like I gave her a shotgun hit, and she's a noob. Her hand flies around her face like she's a smoke ninja and can karate chop air into submission.

There's no smoke around her.

I was courteous.

"Can you not smoke in the truck?" Terra asks. I shake my head no and pack myself up another hit. On my next exhale, Terra coughs like I'm chain-smoking cigarettes and she for sure has lung cancer. Ben cracks his window to appease Terra, and the imaginary killer smoke escapes into the breeze.

I lean my head against the glass and let the cold air from the cracked window drift over my head as my high settles in. It's a blue-bird sun-shiny day outside, which is a direct contrast to the darkness of the night when I last drove down these country roads like a bat out of hell.

Ben is driving a solid ten miles per hour below the speed limit. He's concerned for deer and his concern is valid because four deer pop out of the woods.

"BAMBI!" Terra shrieks and points like she thought Bambi was only a two-dimensional cartoon, and she just witnessed magic.

"Do you guys seem them!?" Terra asks at an unnecessarily loud volume, considering the close quarters. The deer are as blatant as road flares. The horizontal line of their backs stand out compared to the vertical lines of the trees. I see them. They see us.

Ben smiles. "Sure do. Looks like there's four of them."

I say nothing. *What else is there to contribute?* The only information I have pertaining to deer is parasitic and not Disney-related.

Terra still has her finger against the windshield pointing at the deer when they frolic away. The deer's white tails are up— flagging that Ben's truck is a threat. We're the monster.

"Oh my God, they are soo cuuute!" Terra exclaims, turning around to watch the deer dart away. She's oblivious to the fact that they are fleeing our vehicle, that they are fleeing us. I bet in her mind the four deer are rendezvousing with another pack of deer at the watering hole.

Ben slows the truck down further to enable Terra to witness the cuteness. This is a happy moment. *Why am I not smiling? Why am I not looking at Bambi?*

Instead, I keep my head pressed against the window, eyes straightforward, and my mind on the night I was last on these roads.

On *that night*. I was at the bar listening to a local rock band when I received a text. I distinctly remember wiping the condensation off my hands from my margarita before pulling my phone out of my pocket. Genevieve dropped me a pin. My brows creased inward in confusion. I told myself I'd call her when the band took a break. I never leave in the middle of a song. Even in a vehicle, I'll continue idling until the song is over. It's disrespectful to shut down and silence someone's artistic expression.

But my phone rang.

Now in the light of day, I wonder what would have

happened if I didn't answer that call. If I waited for the set to end like I normally would. *Who would be dead?*

Trees blur like someone smeared their palm across a fresh oil painting.

I didn't miss Genevieve's call. I didn't want to brush aside an opportunity to listen to Genevieve's sweet voice beckon me back to worship. Like with most religions, it's instinctive to answer the call. And I felt devout to her. Still do, even though my faith is questioned.

Ben's truck signals a left turn where my car had originally flown by Scarlet Drive. I can scarcely see the tread marks from when I turned around in someone's plot of farmland. Deep grooves and tussled dirt ruin potential crops.

Scarlet Drive has no streetlights. I could have gone for miles without seeing a driveway or road to turn around. I appreciate that about long, winding, country roads. It's a silent fuck you to the city folk. If you don't know where you're going, then you don't belong in these parts. No light will guide your way. The street signs will be a size seven font and faded. And everywhere you go will smell like cow shit. Welcome. Welcome to the country. The land of the free and I don't give a fuck, I own a gun.

Ben signals another left turn onto a long gravel driveway. And keeping consistent with his slow pace, Ben drives ten miles per hour. We drive through a wooded plot for about a mile before we reach the charred ground of what used to be a cabin. The truck rocks to a stop and the first decent song silences mid-chorus.

Ben and Terra hop out of the driver's side door.

"We're here," Ben says clarifying for me as though the mass exodus didn't make it obvious that it's time to disembark from the truck. He's holding onto the doorframe. My fingers itch to turn on the radio.

Outside, the wind tosses up my hair and throws it back in my face. Terra is already off skipping through the trees like she's searching for her lost Border Collie. Ben moves at a more amble pace like he's searching for morel mushrooms and not an over-six-foot-tall man.

I circle the plot of land that the cabin used to sit on as if it might still be on fire.

When I crouch down, the ground isn't warm. My hand feels like it's touching an embalmed body of a relative I'm used to seeing alive and vivacious. In a casket, bodies are frozen—they appear to be napping peacefully, but in reality, they're caked up ice blocks waiting to be gradually lowered six feet under. The juxtaposition of seeing a loved one and touching their hand hoping to wake them up and ultimately feeling chilling rigor mortis is jarring. That's how I feel as I crouch down and sink my fingers into the dirt. Jarred—ripped off and lied to.

I lower myself to my knees and lift my gaze from the dirt to take in the remaining destruction left behind.

My fingers curl as I remember the chaos like a whiplash. I remember the phone call I wasn't planning on answering. I remember Genevieve.

"Hey beautiful," I said with a finger pressed in my opposite ear. I couldn't hear her voice. At first, I thought it was because of the band. It wasn't. Crashing sticks and pain was what I heard. And not drumsticks, I heard physical sticks. Cries and thuds. Panic. Fucking Panic.

I raced to my car and pulled up the pin she dropped. Scarlet Drive? Where the fuck was Scarlet Drive?

I should have gotten in an accident. I should have killed Bambi or multiple Bambis. I got lost and spun around, then spun around again. I don't remember actually driving. My calls dropped. Service was shit. I had trouble understanding Genevieve, I kept saying, "I'm on my way, I'm on my way. I'm almost there." I was fucking lying. I couldn't figure my way out of a box—there were no corners, the reality was a blur, I remember spinning.

*Seconds felt like minutes and minutes felt like hours. "Where
are you?" I asked, full to the brim with anxiety. Her words were
no longer words, just cries, and excruciating noises. So I kept
talking to fill the void.*

*"I'm here—Wait, no I'm not—Where the fuck are you—
Alright, here I am. I think—stand by the road."*

"Wait for me."

"I'm here."

"I'm here."

I WASN'T FAST ENOUGH.

The damage was done before I found my way to Genevieve
—there was no salvation for either of us.

My goddess was wounded.

I don't know how long I'm kneeling with my fingers clawed
deep in the dirt before I start to cry.

My thoughts are paralyzing.

That night was like a car accident. There was no fore-
thought, just instinct. Everything was fine. I stayed in my lane.
Until suddenly, an obstacle that was once yards away became a
few centimeters away. I didn't have time to think. I couldn't
adjust to the change in distance. I only had time to act in a knee
jerk reaction. A tug. A breath. Not even a prayer. Just move.
Knee. Jerk.

Crash.

I'm paralyzed in that knee jerk anxiety.

A collision is inevitable. My concern should be damage
control. But it's not. I'm shaking with tears dripping down and
off my face.

Clap.

A bright light shoots across the sky in a bolt.

Ben appears in my sight with tears coursing down his
face too.

"Aviana," he says grabbing onto my hands and pulling them out of the dirt and pulling me up to my feet.

Our clothing is a second skin. Not just his face is wet, but his whole body is wet. My whole body is wet. Thunder booms. It's pouring rain. I missed the rapidly rising cumulous cloud formations. I missed the darkening sky. I didn't even notice the approach.

Ben pushes me into the truck and slams the passenger door shut behind me. He runs around the front of the truck to his side and shuts the driver's side door with force. My seat is sodden wet—I never closed the window. Terra sits with her knees pulled up to her chest. She's dry, sitting in the middle of the cab. Ben shakes his head like a dog. Terra shrieks and tucks herself into her knees to avoid the water. *How long was Ben trying to get me to move?* The expanse between us feels like miles.

My thoughts are still outside in the past while my body is physically in the truck.

"Fuck," Ben shouts. He looks over at me like he's seeing me for the very first time.

The truck roars to life, and the radio blasts from the volume Terra left it on. Ben quickly turns the radio down to a coffee shop appropriate level. This is no longer an adventure.

"Aviana, close the window," Ben whispers before shifting gears into drive.

"What's wrong with her?" Terra whispers to Ben like I'm not in the truck's cab with them. Maybe Terra senses the miles of distance too.

"Nothing, there's nothing wrong with her."

A few minutes pass and Ben reminds me again to close the window. Rain pelts against the glass as it rises to its seal. Drops drip across the rim like an infinity pool.

The day disappeared. It was a bluebird day until I lost track of time in my thoughts. *How did it happen that fast?*

Or was it even fast at all?

I'm ready to strangle Terra after the second day of her visit. The woman tosses out ideas that someone abducted Hudson and we should seek paranormal experts to help track him down. She continually drops proverbial business cards as though she's receiving a commission. Why haven't we called 1-888-P5YCH1C? Why aren't we part of her paranormal chatroom? We should be in this group text. The thread is trending and I'm behind with a dead phone that I'm not rushed to charge.

At dinner, two weeks after Hudson's disappearance, desperation clogs the air. Everything we haven't said out loud smog's the air like New York traffic.

I move my vegetables around my plate—my appetite is gone. Peas roll around like bowling balls, plowing and getting congested in mashed potatoes. Silverware *clink* and *clack* like handcuffs.

"How do we even know Hudson was in the cabin?" Terra asks behind a napkin.

Ben is still chewing and I ignore her while my fork guides my peas around my plate.

Terra adds on, "And why haven't we talked to Genevieve?"

"We have already questioned her," I say to my peas because I don't want to look at Terra's face.

"Genevieve is a delicate subject with both of us. It's best if you would drop it," Ben says, looking back and forth between the both of us. He sits at the head of the table with one of us on each side. He looks left, right, then left again to really give me a good eyeful. He wears a well-worn expression, like he's a sad father consoling a teenage girl who won't stop rebelling against the very air her mother breathes. He wants to get rid of the bickering. His crisp tone makes that abundantly clear. And the fact that he told us made it crystal.

"I still don't understand why you never took Hudson with you that night," Terra comments towards me. The piercing glare Terra receives is from Ben. It's a parent's glare that says *knock it off* without uttering a word.

Terra folds her napkin down onto the table and says, "I just don't understand how someone in their right mind wouldn't turn around and at least check on him. The building was burning down for Christ's sake."

She leans forward across the table and gets into my personal space. "Weren't you at all concerned? We're you even dating? Do you even care? You're not even here." She looks to Ben for confirmation. "She's physically here, but is she *really*?"

Ben's chair noisily slides back. He leaves in a huff. Terra makes a move to leave, but her words leash her to me. She's moving just for show. She knows she has me. She's as tethered to me as I am to her and won't leave until she says what she has to say. I won't leave until I hear it. I want to know.

"What happened between you and Hudson the last couple of days he was around?" I whisper. I lift my gaze from my plate. Terra sits directly in front of me with all her exotic curves. I wish my whispers were roars.

She leans back against the support of her chair in thought. Her fingers clutch her necklace. The sound of her sliding the pendant against the thin chain sounds like a slithering snake's tongue as it cases the air, *hissing*—it burrows into my ear canal. The grind slithers under my skin each time. Every other minute, her fingers are twiddling and sliding around the heart-shaped pendant.

I try to keep my responding twitch to myself, but it inevitably turns into my own disgusting habit. My twitch is Pavlov's dog to her fucking heart.

"He gave me back my necklace. He kept it all this time. Isn't that the sweetest?" Terra's voice is whiskey smooth. It lulls me into listening, into wanting to listen.

She isn't waiting for my response—she's off in her head with her whimsical version of Hudson. Her eyes focus on me like she can't understand why I haven't upgraded to her cloud nine.

I can't argue with her, I'm disappointing myself too.

"He gave me back his heart."

3

POLICE REPORT

At 2210 hours on Sunday, 30 October 2011, I, Officer Dale Shepherd #721, was dispatched to investigate a structure fire at 850 Scarlet Drive, Viola; a wood-frame construction, single-story, one-family residence.

While en route, I was informed by responder Nancy Creekwater that a WF was admitted to Saint Catherine's Hospital at 2220 hours—victim of aggravated assault. The assailant was last seen at dispatched address. I was advised to proceed with caution.

Engine 4 was first to arrive on the scene and reported an active fire at 2225 hours. The fire crew went on the offensive attack and controlled, then extinguished the fire. Captain Gary Frasier reported the fire resulted in complete destruction of the structure. No civilian victims were found in the interior of the fire. The structure was not fitted with an automatic fire sprinkler system.

I conducted an initial scene survey and saw evidence of extreme heat and fast spreading fire. The overhead of the front of the structure was completely destroyed and had fallen into the areas it once covered. There was thick charring in the remaining roof structure. I saw no evidence of fuel or accelerant. There was no furniture in the structure. No other evidence as to the cause of the fire was found. No witnesses were at the scene. The alleged suspect, Hudson Thomas' SUV was left at the scene.

At 0147 hours on Monday, 31 October 2011, I, Officer Shepherd went to Saint Catherine's Hospital to interview the potential witnesses. The victim of aggravated assault, a WF, Genevieve Porter was admitted to Saint Catherine's Hospital, room 330. Her eye makeup was streaked and smeared on her wet face. Her lips were trembling. Red marks were scattered along her skin with no specific target zone.

She (Genevieve Porter) said that Hudson Thomas attacked her. Aviana Whitaker picked her up from 850 Scarlet Drive, Viola, on Sunday, 30 October 2011. Whitaker stated she transported the victim directly from the scene of the incident to the hospital where the victim was registered at 2220 hours. Whitaker stayed in the room during questioning but refused any further comment outside of demanding a new room.

Genevieve Porter stated Hudson Thomas contacted her the week prior and requested to pick her up for assistance at the alleged residence on Scarlet Drive. He requested she not tell Aviana Whitaker. Thomas and Whitaker were in an alleged relationship. Porter indicated Thomas was running late and offered to buy dinner at Chipotle. After their meal, Thomas drove them to the residence on Scarlet Drive. Inside the vehicle during the drive, Thomas revealed he had recently purchased the residence on Scarlet Drive. Once inside the residence, Thomas presented mural and mosaic tiling options. He requested Porter's opinion. Porter stated she was looking through mosaics when Thomas abruptly knocked Porter down in the living room. Porter described that Thomas did not make any noises throughout the attack.

She stated, "He overpowered me from behind like a coward. He just kept beating and kicking me until I stopped defending myself. Then he watched me crawl to the front door. Anytime I rolled to my knees or tried to rise, he would kick me, or push me down."

When asked how she escaped, Porter stated, "He let me leave. He could have chased me and he didn't. I slammed the door and ran."

When asked how the fire originated, Porter had no remembrance. Porter also could not recollect specifically what Thomas was wearing, she stated, "Jeans and a dark colored t-shirt."

Due to the nature of the attack, Porter never saw the assailant, nor did she turn back and verify Thomas' identity during the escape.

WORKING timeline after speaking with Genevieve Porter:

1945 hours Thomas picked up Porter from her apartment residence.

2005 hours Thomas paid for dinner for both Porter and himself at Chipotle.

2058 hours Thomas and Porter arrived at the residence.

2210 hours Whitaker contacted 911 dispatcher and reported the fire.

2220 hours Whitaker and Porter arrived at the hospital.

CLINICAL PRESENTATION OF GENEVIEVE PORTER: multiple fractures to her left and right ribs, fractured skull, a dislocated jaw, surface lacerations across her extremities, a broken right forearm, sprained a left ankle, blackened right eye and various internal injuries.

. . .

THE ALLEGED SUSPECT, Hudson Thomas, could not be found for questioning.

Aviana Whitaker refused medical treatment.

AT 1000 HOURS TUESDAY, 1 November 2011, I, Officer Shepherd, visited Genevieve Porter at Saint Catherine's Hospital, room 501. I went over her statement and asked if she had anything to add. Porter had nothing to add to her statement. Intense pain, swelling, and extensive bruising kept Porter in an uncooperative, medically induced disposition. The medical staff advised against further questioning.

At 1415 hours I recovered Genevieve Porter's phone records from Monday, 1 November:

1900 call received from Hudson Thomas.
Call duration 5 minutes.
1945 call received from Hudson Thomas.
Call duration 30 seconds.
2134 call sent to Aviana Whitaker.
Call duration 10 minutes.
2154 call received from Aviana Whitaker.
Call duration 48 seconds.
2156 call received from Aviana Whitaker.
Call duration 20 seconds.
2157 call received from Aviana Whitaker.
Call duration 10 seconds.

At 1817 hours I transferred the case to Detective Norman. No new information has been received on the whereabouts of suspect Hudson Thomas.

THREE MONTHS AGO

4

FAITH IN RELIGION ONLY REQUIRES BELIEF

THE CLOCK STRIKES ten at night. Howls from the wind get shut out behind me as I close the door.

Lights are on. With a flick of my wrist, the lock slides into place.

I stand still and listen—she's here.

I stand still and wait—she'll come for me. She's restless of my growing affection towards Hudson.

It isn't hard to read her, just like it isn't hard to read me. The evidence is in her tense shoulders, her jealous smirk, her narrowed eyes. All of which are directed at me.

I'm the mouse to her cat, and I don't mind being caught. In fact, I prefer it. *Come here, pussy.*

My bookbag thumps to the floor, its contents jostle within the fabric. I stay leaning against the front door and watch her approach. My eyes creep up from her red toenails, over the fine lines of her exquisite body, and finally rest on her piercing brown eyes. Her gaze is a warm **Welcome Home**.

I've never really felt religion. I've never truly felt connected. But then I met Genevieve.

She consumes me. She gives me hope and absolves my sins.

I find the freedom to be my unadulterated self within her

arms, on the tip of her tongue and with her flat on her back. I'd give anything to hear the hitch in her breath when I touch her just right.

To say she's mine would be a lie, but to say I am hers would be divine.

Her red toenails stop parallel to my sneaker covered ones. It's been weeks since our schedules aligned and we were in the same room together.

The moment feels like a tape deck being rewound.

"I've missed you, who's been keeping you from me?" Genevieve asks, bringing the entanglement of our hands to her lips. My hunger for her flips a switch to need. She bites lightly down on my index finger, lifting it to rest idly on her bottom lip.

"No one has been keeping me. I've been alone in the library."

My finger slides across the curves of her lips as they separate to say, "You should be here with me."

I sizzle like a drop of water splashing onto a scalding hot frying pan. "You're too distracting." Genevieve is a sight for my sore eyes in her purple silk robe that hovers against her upper thighs.

"Well, I suppose you're done studying, and it's time to play." Genevieve withdraws her hand from mine and skips into the kitchen. She reappears moments later with two bottles of wine and two freshly rolled blunts. We spend the few remaining hours of night drinking and smoking.

It's a little after midnight and Genevieve won't let me touch her, no matter how many advances I make. We're sitting on the couch watching a documentary on survivalists. So far, I've learned that preppers stash tampons and maxi pads. Aside from their obvious functions, female sanitary products can be used as sterile dressings for wounds, compresses, or bartering.

My attention fades once the host goes over the many uses of kitty litter. *Who knew?* I didn't and still don't.

Instead, I focus on Genevieve and wonder if her cold shoulder is my reprimand for not being in her company—a punishment for not making her my priority.

I run my knuckles up and down her arm. Time and time again she's told me I need to be there for her. I need to be here, physically *here*. But she needs to understand that sixty-nine is a dinner for two and I'm famished. I lean across her and smash the blunt in the ashtray. My skin is tight and stretched too thin. I'm an unwilling participant in a waiting game, and I don't understand how to play. Nor do I want to learn the rules.

I push and pin Genevieve into the leather cushions beneath us. My arms bracket her straight as jail bars on either side of her face. Liquid fire fuels my veins in a circuit throughout my body.

I lean forward and press my mouth forcefully against hers. I reconnect myself with her— get her taste on my tongue. She undulates and rolls into me like a wave of pleasure against my shore.

"Wicked woman," I say haughtily against her lips. Her breath becomes my next.

A soft laugh erupts from my pinned companion, followed by a forceful hand that pushes me back— releasing her imprisonment.

"I'm not done with you. Go buy more wine." She squints at the clock. "It's not time."

I gawk back at her. I shouldn't have to drive. "I can barely walk."

Her soft pink lipstick is smudged on her lips, most likely across mine too. I bite my bottom lip and taste her.

"Go to the corner carry-out. I can't go. I'm only wearing my robe."

Looking down at myself in my black tank top and torn-up jeans, I debate undressing and throwing her logic back at her like an intoxicated boomerang. Maybe she'll pull a monkey-see-monkey-do and drop the robe.

Her stare is telling me different.

Frustrated and ever yearning for affection, I let out a sigh of accordance and continue to be Genevieve's pawn. I snatch my wallet and head out the door.

PAST THE POINT of no return, the intoxication train I'm on is full steam ahead.

An hour later, I return after having an animated conversation with the owner of the corner carry-out, something about phone cards and ice cream. Pretty sure I was the butt-end to each of his jokes.

My arms are full with bags. Come to think of it, our conversation might have been about lottery tickets and black tea. My left hand holds a wooden stick. I drop exhibit A in the trash and lick my sweetened lips.

In the kitchen, I recall laughing with my full body at the register. I recall pushing my credit card into the reader and accepting a thirty-dollar charge. I recall saying farewell to Mark. Or was it Mohammed? Moe? Morgan? No name sounds right. I know it has two syllables and starts with an 'M'. At least I think I do. *M*...

Knocks at the front door interrupt my thoughts.

A fist demands acknowledgment three times. I know this because I count three very succinct knocks that if personified would ask *beg your pardon?*

My head snaps right. *Who could that be?*

Just as 'the fuck', in *who the fuck is there?* —leaves my mouth, the door opens towards me.

My foot lifts from the pedal and the lid to the trashcan taps closed. All I see is wood and Genevieve. I watch her lean against the door, the amethyst silk slides up. I wait for the punch of color, yet see only round naked ass cheeks. No underwear in sight. Everything within my arms gets an immediate drop off on the counter. Simply the thought of touching Genevieve's soft skin has a shiver racing down my spine. I rub my hands together. I'm equal parts excited and wasted.

Her giggle has me expanding my awareness parameters to just outside her ass. I'm torn between looking up and acknowledging the intruder I forgot about and walking forwards and grabbing a handful.

Having my cake and eating it too, I look up as I step forward. Head and shoulders rise above Genevieve. My palm touches ass-cheek. My eyes simultaneously connect to a pair of yellow irises that could only belong to Hudson. *Hudson?*

My brain drips. *What the fuck?*

Genevieve's giggle continues into the interior of our apartment. She has Hudson by the wrist. I'm pushed behind the door to make way.

Genevieve promptly begins chirping from her high pedestal of conspiracy. I push the door and it slams closed.

My tongue is incapable of speech, my mouth is bone dry.

I'm at a clear disadvantage.

All eyes are on Genevieve. This is her moment to shine and make this look nice.

She walks through the living room like a flight attendant rambling about important information I should listen to. I'm that asshole passenger sitting next to an emergency exit that doesn't read the special instruction card. I do not wish to perform the functions described in the event of an emergency, and I don't ask the flight attendant to reseat me.

She continues to lead Hudson by the wrist away from me.

Her golden locks and Ms. American smile lead me down

past the couch and patio doors. I follow her because that's what I do. *Why would I do any differently?*

I willingly give her my wheel.

I STAND in front of a large white oak dresser with an obscenely large white ornate mirror. The mirror is narrow and almost reaches the ceiling. It looks like a portal for giants.

Across the bottom corner of the mirror is my reflection. I stare back at myself with wide eyes. The turquoise hue of my irises are bold and gem-like against my pale skin and dark hair. Bright pink walls are my background. Oversized white furniture and shocking walls. The room is the perfect backdrop for a doll-house fetish.

My fingers clutch around the white dresser's edge as I take in the scene developing behind me. Genevieve's hands won't leave Hudson alone. They're touching his fingers, then traveling up to his forearm. One hand presses against his chest.

A flash catches my eye. A tiny orange flame expands and turns into smoke as a fresh blunt is sparked. Hudson's eyes flick to mine through the smoke in the mirror's reflection. It lasts only a moment, but he asks me a million questions. I ask him a million more.

"Explain the game again," Hudson says to Genevieve. His voice pulls at my drowned resistance. I'm simultaneously floating and sinking. My feet have cement shoes, but my head is gaseous.

What game?

Hudson and Genevieve continue talking. A majority of their words reach my ears like the words from the adults in Charlie Brown; '*Wah, wah, wah*'. I try to focus, but there is a significant error in translation.

I'm barely here.

I'm mostly sensation.

"... more of a play date," Genevieve says sauntering towards me. Hypnotizing hips swaying.

I reach out like a well-deserving student. My hand hits the mirror. *Fucking moron.* I turn around and cup my hand to my chest.

Genevieve makes more sense the closer to me she comes. I want to play—I've been begging—*I want to play with her.* She's my favorite toy and I've been waiting all night.

Genevieve moves in front of me. The air between us disappears and I finally sense her warmth. It blankets me and soothes my ripped, ragged, raw edges. Genevieve kisses me generously across my collarbone. I tip my head back and watch the wood panels of the fan sift the heated air. Between the whirl in the soft pads of her fingers and the whirling sounds emitted from the fan, I'm possessed. Helpless to stop this act, even if I wanted to. I don't.

I surrender to her rose velvet touch. I dismiss all spoken words. I want to decipher the phrases licked. I want to be fluent in the language of Genevieve.

Feminine hands pull me closer. I let out a hum of satisfaction and close my eyes. I feel like such a good girl. I want it to stay this way, at least for tonight.

My fingers dig deep into the soft flesh of her hips. The silk fabric of her robe bunches in my grip before fluttering down her curves. I pull her head up to mine, and I breathe into her ear; "Let me have you."

Genevieve vibrates.

She is either laughing or talking loudly. Either way, it feels at my expense.

She pulls away from me.

I stagger back a step and hit the dresser. I feel less than human. My heart jumps. My eyes open long enough to grab and drag her back to me.

Fuck that.

No more waiting. Now is a great time. No time like the present for a present. I'm sure I'll come to my senses when I'm sober. But right now, I'm ripping her purple wrapping. Right now, I'm getting the dessert I've craved all night. At this moment, I'm in heaven.

My breath heaves as I unveil a body so proportionately equivalent to Barbie it should give me a complex. I reverently cup Genevieve's large breasts in my hands and massage them in rhythm to the aching between my legs. I bring my mouth down to her neck and press her backward. She hits the dresser with a shocked noise I don't pay attention to. Our safe word is 'Beetle-juice', and she isn't saying any words that are remotely three syllables long. I grab her from behind her knees and toss her up on her grandiose dresser. I might as well be deaf—I am only listening to her body, and her body fucking missed me.

She knots her fingers in my hair and forces my head against her right breast. I swirl my tongue along her nipple until it rises to the occasion. Her fists cage me against her body. She controls me, and I release myself to her willingly. I am blissfully okay with her command on me, I take what I'm being given.

Genevieve is highly vocal, almost to a show-stopping applause. With a sense of the dramatic, fully nude, she is breath-taking. She knows it.

Being her number one fan, I encourage her. My kisses are petals at her altar.

My hand lowers between her V and presses hard. I'm no longer in my skin. I'm deep in her.

She grinds against me, lubricating my palm.

My knees drop to the carpet. I pull her hips towards the edge, towards my mouth. The angel wings tattooed above Genevieve's clit glistens.

I pay tribute to her alter. I'm overdressed for the occasion, I still have on a black tank top and ripped jeans. At least I took my shoes off at the door when I came home from the store. Or maybe my shoes are in the kitchen. Either way, they're off my feet. I'm off my feet. I'm on bended knees.

Loud moans escape Genevieve. I watch her in a trance from my position.

She playfully circles her own hardened nipple. Fondling her breast, she gasps on a cry of pleasure and climaxes staring behind me.

Genevieve pulls me up by my hair and grasps my chin with her previously playful hand. She kisses me in appreciation. I try to wrap my arms around her, but she stands firm and I'm pushed aside aggressively.

Teetering and almost on my ass, I wipe her saliva and juices off my face.

Genevieve doesn't even bother to slip her robe back on. Her hips sashay from side to side. Her sinuous body strides down a carpeted runway seductively over to Hudson.

Hudson is still here.

Embarrassment steams out of my ears and dries my vocal cords. He sits at the windowsill with a half-drunk red wine bottle at his boots. A partially smoked blunt between his lips. His predatory eyes flare like tinder set aflame.

Genevieve snatches the waning blunt from his lips and sucks smoothly on the sweet smoke. Her body blocks most of my view of him. Her upturned chin hides his gaze.

He reaches for the blunt.

Genevieve's breast stops his hand; her hard nipple is still moist from our combined saliva. She leans forward like she's going to give him mouth to mouth. Her hand pushes on his chest. She presses his body against the window. The curvaceous body I just paid homage to is a turncoat.

Smoke escapes through the gaps of their lips.

Her shotgun exhale erupts and magnifies in my mind like a series of bombs. This can't be happening.

Once more, Genevieve's mouth brushes against his lips like she's mourning the loss of his taste.

I stand there, staring at his mouth. She got to taste him before me. He's in her bloodstream.

Genevieve pulls Hudson's hand away from his lap and presses his hand down her sternum. Over her belly button. And introduces his hand to her wings.

5

MY LION'S ROAR IS QUIET

A SOFT KNOCK rasps at my bedroom door.

"Go away!" I yell somewhat incoherently from beneath a pillow. I'm not sure how much time elapsed since I've left Genevieve's bedroom. Time is a variable; I can interchange its value with any second, minute, or hour. Time holds no meaning without a relationship to a constant. And nothing is consistent in this reality. Reality itself is being questioned.

The door is unlocked and opens on its own volition. I should've locked it. Abruptly someone confiscates the pillow over my head. Hudson stands at my bedside and he's angry. He has no right to be angry, but he looks fucking pissed. Dually pissed—as in very annoyed, angry, and British properly drunk. He tosses the pillow behind him. Darkness swallows it.

I sit up with venom poised on the tip of my tongue. "What the fuck are you doing here?" I ask looking anywhere but at him. I hope my words come out like missiles. From my peripheral, I see his expression and it's clear that I'm slinging sluggish shit. *Am I even making words?*

I stare across my room and out the windows. The dimensions are like Genevieve's room. Except, instead of the nook, I have four windows that comprise the far wall.

Silence.

Nothing in my room moves but the shadows of moonlit branches and green leaves.

His voice hits my right ear first. "Yesterday-"

"Fuck. Off."

He looks up to the ceiling like it will split in two and wisdom will rain upon him. "Yesterday when you called me."

"I didn't fucking call you," I whisper-yell. We sound like children trying to keep our voices down so Mommy Dearest doesn't barge in.

Hudson's head snaps down, but before I'm able to catch his gaze he spins. His arm rises to punch the wall. His fist is inches from the lavender paint when it opens and slaps the wall instead. His head taps against the wall like he's trying to buzz himself in. But I'm not responsive.

"This was supposed to be a game. A very erotic game," he says turning back to me. "The call was from your phone." His gaze softens, "I thought it was you who finally invited me over. I thought it was you who finally broke down to reveal your supposed dream—a dream that included me meeting your needs. Where you took me Av. You came for me." He stops for a moment, gathering his thoughts. "When I got here, Genevieve was in my face. She reiterated something about a game with fucked up rules. I wasn't supposed to look at you. I wasn't supposed to talk to you. All I could do was wait. I thought you were in on it. I thought you would come *to me*." He snorts a breath that pretty much calls himself out as an idiot. "Honestly Av, I didn't give a fuck. Genevieve was my connection to you. She had you. *She fucking had you.* And you couldn't keep your eyes off of her."

He's right, but how can that be held against me? *What are we even arguing about?*

His eyes implore me. "Who the fuck is she to you?"

"Who the fuck is she to you? You kissed her." *She's in you —in US.*

"For you to watch. I thought that's what you're into. That's what this whole fucking night is about. What the fuck Av?"

What the fuck.

My face falls against my knees. My skin is entirely too sensitive. He doesn't quite touch me, but he stands close enough that the heat of his body is against mine.

"I came here to be with you. I want you."

This isn't how it's supposed to happen. I think to myself. Or I might have said it out loud. Regardless, I do say, "I want you to leave." I know this because of his reaction.

Abruptly he backs up as if I hit him. He paces the room at a loss with his explanations or lack thereof. His hands rake through his hair leaving a ten-fingered style. Curls from his mane stand askew at all ends. He prowls like the lion he appears to be.

I watch his movements between the gaps of my fingers. Multiple Hudsons track my floor, frame-by-frame, then snap back into one form.

The room turns on its axis. *Is this going to be the last time I speak to Hudson?* Awkwardness is a third person in the room. Everyone is watching me, all illusionary and 3D versions.

He reverts to hand gestures and shows the space between us. "We can't solve anything tonight."

His eyes question me. *Why can't I see the gameplay he reveals before us?* I see nothing but dead air.

"Why are you still here?" I whisper.

A few moments pass and I turn my head slightly to peer at him with one eye and one raised eyebrow.

In front of me he stands like an all-American hero, drained, exhausted from battle. All he wants is to come home. *Why won't I open the door? Why won't I let him in? Am I not an American?*

"This isn't how it's supposed to happen," he says crumbling

to the floor, his back against the bed frame, "and I don't want to go. I don't want to leave us like this." He waves his hand from him to me, showing the participants of 'us'. Except I'm behind him, so it looks like he's jacking off the air above him.

"Us?" I shriek in a high pitched whisper. There is no us. There has never been an us.

His head drops between his shoulders. He mutters a torrent of words and phrases that might have been apologies to him, to me, or the universe. I need more hand gestures or to read his lips. *What happened to the game plan?*

He moves in the space of an instant and my brain lollygags behind him.

On the bed and crowding me with his much larger body against mine, he says, "there is an us." His words come out as a rumbling growl—like I should have fucking known better.

Complete blackness looks back at me. The pupil of each of his eyes stretches across, covering the iris and sclera of each respective space.

He quickly turns away, shameful, covering his face with his hands.

"Your eyes...", comes out as a gasp—I'm straddling two worlds.

Our eye contact is over like a gunshot. Quick, sobering, and painful. And like a gunshot, it changes everything. It creates a marker. A pre-and-post-confession. Neither of us says anything as the smoke clears and our thoughts take form.

HUDSON SITS with his back against the headboard. I sit up. We're shoulder to shoulder.

"Why didn't you run away?"

This is the Hudson I know, quiet and pensive. My hand reaches and grasps his for only a moment before letting go.

"I'm not like most," I whisper back.

"No, you're not."

I wonder more about how he came to be here tonight. I wonder what happened when I left Genevieve's bedroom. But what interests me most are his eyes and their effect on me. And why are they now a normal golden yellow and not swathed in pitch black? All of these questions and more swim around in my consciousness, but what I ask out loud is, "You won't let anything bad happen to me, will you, Hudson?"

My heart does a nervous somersault. My inhibitions are nonexistent. I just need a strong wind to fall into him.

There's a faraway look to Hudson's whiskey eyes.

I reach out with both of my hands and cradle his face. My touch seems to anchor him. His eyes clear. I move closer. I want to be anchored too.

I lean my forehead against his, offering both a challenge and prayer within a single breath. My lips tip to his and move in slow motion. I press a feather-light request to be a little more connected. A little more connected to him.

His body clenches, tightening in every muscle. He swallows hard. *Is he as painfully aware as I am? Can he sense how much I'm allowing myself to give him?*

Again, my lips brush along his full counterparts. And again, and again. With each brush, I stay a little longer, press a little harder.

He wraps one arm around my back and pulls me tight against his chest. The heat of his body sears me. Aggressively, he presses my body into him, he can't get close enough. His fingers move and dig roughly into my hips.

I kiss him with a yearning to understand if he's worth me. I kiss him with a desire to let go of the secrets I shoulder. And with each press of our lips the hardback cover of my story opens, my lips separate and I let him read my pages and taste my words.

I tap into a part of myself that I normally can't reach without assistance. It's the part of me that is sealed tight and requires an exorcism to loosen the lid.

Hudson's smoldering voice creeps, "Aviana." His voice is distant, as if he calls to me from the opposite end of an underground tunnel. The sound of his voice in my mind startles me back to reality, or as close to reality as I can get.

Did I just hear his voice in my head?

I lean away from him and I see wonder widen his eyes.

We are two of a kind. Darkness consumes my eyes too. His set of blackened eyes stare back at mine in a Mexican standoff, our weapons loaded. His breath puffs against my jaw.

Dull light seeps through the windows bathing us.

"Can I stay with you tonight?"

I nod...

Words... words have left me.

His fingers lower and inch my tank top higher to rest below my shoulder blades. His fingers dance along my skin. He scrolls a language only he can decipher along my back.

My head rests heavily on his chest. A deep flowing rush echoes in my ear. His heart pumps a lullaby, sounding like my personal ocean. I'm a stone in his waters. Sunk deep. I don't respond when he asks, "Do you think there are others like us?"

FOGGY AND CRIPPLED by a hazy confusion of the last twelve hours—my mouth smacks as though I swallowed cotton balls for all three meals. My left arm is numb and folded beneath me. My naked right leg is strewn across jean-clad legs.

Fully waking, my eyes open and I see a soft gray horizon rise and fall. The full-day floods into my bedroom. Last night's revelations crash down on me like a line of dominoes.

Tinkering and clanking of plates from the kitchen trigger me to propel out of bed and pull on my green and gray flannel robe. Hudson doesn't wake up. He doesn't even move. He looks expansive and utterly relaxed. His hands remain above his head as if I handcuffed him. It's a good look on him. I shut the door.

"Good Morning sunshine," Genevieve says as she continues to clang pots and pans from the dishwasher. She tosses them inside the cabinets, causing more ruckus. I place my hand over hers and nonverbally tell her to stop her parade of sensory pain. Delusional from the overload, I release my grip from her and wish my rowdy roommate a good morning.

Genevieve slams the cabinets closed and pours two mugs of coffee. "You scampered off to bed quickly. I thought you would have wanted to stay up with Hudson and I. Cream and sugar?"

"Sugar, please." I fold into a kitchen chair debating if I want to rip into her or bite my tongue maintaining my squatters' rights. The apartment is leased only to one tenant, Genevieve. And she knows how I like my fucking coffee. She's diverting from her shtick. Going off script, forcing my words.

"So..." she encourages.

I clasp the mug in my hands and take a small sip of the sweetened black liquid.

"Did you drink too much wine?" She inquires behind her mug that's branded with the name of a local hotel chain. It's beige and dull. Her mug looks as though it once had all the intentions of remaining white, yet tarnished with time and stains.

"I suppose so."

"It wasn't out of jealousy?"

"No, but do you care to explain yourself?" Of course, I'm jealous. I'm an array of emotions. But Genevieve doesn't need to understand, she doesn't need to learn any more. She's evicted from my personal business. *What the fuck was last night?* That's what I want to learn. But I also want a roof and a bed. I need to be patient when handling Genevieve. I need to act with tact and remember that like her mug, she currently holds me and can easily break my beige ass.

"I thought he could play well with us," she says like its plenty explanation. Now it's up to me if make-up sex is on the table. Literally, she hops up on the table and maneuvers herself so I'm between her legs. Her heels rest on either side of my chair.

"Through ambush? You should have called him to us and not have gone to him," I say, not accepting her excuse.

"I thought he was just your friend. It shouldn't matter if I fuck him or not if he wants to." She takes a healthy sip of coffee, "and he wanted to."

She's giving me her two-cents from a pellet gun aimed straight at my chest. The tiny marbles of facts are piercing.

The power position she's sitting in has me looking up to her to respond. I could look straightforward and respond to her snatch, but it isn't her vagina's fault that she was a cunt last night. "I thought it was just going to be the both of us. If I had known he would be here last night, I wouldn't have been that fucked up. I couldn't function and you sent me out for more. And don't even get me started on the ceaseless teasing. You played me."

"And you play such beautiful music," she says coldly. It's abundantly clear that I'm to blame for her current attitude. I took sex off the table. *What is my purpose?* She's back in her chair and glaring at me.

"Don't do it again, not with Hudson."

Her arms cross against her chest, "possessive are we?"

"I can't control him," Genevieve leans back like a queen in her throne. "I've never seen you fight for anyone before."

She's taking my measure. I feel her dicing stare as she

disseminates every hostile term mentioned between us. Our chemistry right now is combustive, and not in a positive sense. I lay my proverbial weapons down and back away. I'm calling off our war to allow my cuts and bruises to heal—a temporary cease of bullshit. Let me stay. Don't break me yet.

A TOURIST'S TRIP

WITH THE WARM mug of coffee between my fingers, I creep silently back to my bedroom. I shed my robe, it falls to the floor. Coffee splashes over the rim when the mug settles on the night-stand. *Click*, I lock the door and slide back into bed.

Vicariously I slip my hand over Hudson's chest. I play with the folds in his thin gray shirt. Sometimes talking to Genevieve is like staring at the sun. You can only see the sun through a side-glance. Staring at the sun long-term may cause partial blindness. It hurts all my sensibilities. I want Genevieve's warmth, her sunshine, and blue skies—not to sweat and drain in her heat. And since she's is hell-bent on meeting me on the front lines, I hide in my bed, back to my dreams with Hudson at my fingertips.

His heart pumps faintly stronger at my light touch. I walk my fingers up his shirt and slice his throat along the collar's edge. Faster, his heart pumps *lub-dub, lub-dub, lub-dub*.

I leave a trail of butterfly kisses along his neck.

Hudson hums and lifts me to straddle his morning wood. My lips brave a new trail along the other side of his neck. My tongue licks the shell of his ear.

His chest rumbles like he's purring.

He pushes me back—we separate—his hands are hot on my skin. He lifts the fabric of my tank top over my head.

The scarf of my hair covers my breasts from Hudson's hungry eyes. He smiles a wolfish grin at me and tucks my hair behind my ears to wisp my tailbone.

He hasn't said a word. Our nonverbal communication is an aphrodisiac.

His hand grips his shirt from behind his head, pulls, and discards the fabric. He does it in a manner that screams he was only wearing a shirt for my comfort—to meet my expectations— shirts are a nuisance.

We meet chest to chest. His hands grip my ass and I nuzzle into his jawline. I agree whole-heartedly with the no shirt clause. Skin to skin is a much better argument. Skin to skin has a far better sensation.

Gray clouds spiral into imaginative figures outside. Shadows dance in the room like uninvited ghosts. Hudson holds me close. My skin is feverish against his touch.

A heavy knock drops on the door. "Aviana, what are you doing? Why is the door locked?" Genevieve yanks on the handle trying to wrench the door open with sheer force. "Don't be mad at me." More wild attempts pursue. "He left alright... He never stayed the night."

Hostility washes over me at the recollection of last night's betrayal. The sensation attacks me like a horde of cartoon hyenas ripping me to shreds while laughing psychotically. Genevieve's body laid draped across Hudson flashes in my memory. We're in the exact same position. Her lips tasted him first. He's in her bloodstream.

Another series of knocks. "It's funny because he told me he would love to... Well, you know." Genevieve slides down the door, her voice lowering with her. "I fell asleep waiting for him to come back. He said he had to piss, and I guess he left."

My body joins my head in shaking. I hate the effect the

memories have on me. I haven't even had time to shit, shower, and shave between Hudson being with Genevieve and the Hudson that is alone with me now.

"Would you care if I called him?" Rain slaps across the windows like a backhand across my face. Eyes swathed in black, I reply, "No..." The change doesn't alter my temperament. Though it surprises me that the change to my eyes happened.

Hudson whispers against my neck, "Don't push me away."

It's too late. I grab my robe and distance myself. I'm inches from the door. My phone is attached to the charger. I walk over to it and read off Hudson's number to Genevieve. The last digits slough off my tongue.

Hudson puts his shirt on, turns off his phone and sets it on the nightstand. He looks at me like it's now my move. *Go.*

"Call him whenever you want." I deadpan.

"Alright, I think I will. I have to go run a few errands... I'll see you later." At her parting words, Genevieve leaves the apartment. We hear her departure with the front door shutting. I wonder how much better she feels because I feel worse. I feel back in the shed I was locked in as a child. The memories run parallel—they're holding hands and skipping to my demise with sharpened knives cutting up my insides for a picnic at the depths of my gut. They stomp around feeling heavy as fuck.

Thunder rumbles under heaven's grip. Hopefully, Genevieve forgot her umbrella. I look back to my bed and slowly make it back to my coffee mug. I take a long drag and hate myself. The liquid is too sweet and now cold. It needs to be hot and bitter, exactly how I feel.

Yet I drink the gross coffee and swallow big bouts of air. I need a reason to stand beside Hudson that isn't complicated. So I stand beside him, but I won't make eye contact. And I stand in silence at the designated drinking station and sip an undrinkable drink.

"Aviana... I thought after last night..." His first words to me this morning are drenched in regret. Thunder grumbles again in the sky.

I can't shake my composure and say, "After last night, this is about this morning, Hudson."

"I've been with you all morning."

I peer over my mug and focus my black eyes on him. His eyes are still molten and a saddened yellow, like a kicked puppy, cue Sarah McLachlan's *Angel*.

"Hudson," I start. I sound like I'm whining, but, "I don't know what to say". I hold up my coffee mug as if it's a part of the conversation. My mug has a glittering unicorn in full gallop. *I'm fucking magical* is scripted with the words floating in the unicorn's wake. Or perhaps out its ass, as if it's farting philosophical glitter. I feel anything but magical. Cursed fits better.

Lightning strikes.

Hudson takes the mug.

"What did I miss this morning?" He asks between sips of the drivel once known as coffee. He makes a displeased face, "this tastes like shit." Indeed.

I shrug, "It upset Genevieve that you left her last night and she wants to have you back. Then she'll throw you aside with the other rejects. She can't handle being told no, but she can't be held down either. She's an addict for the chase and wants to be loved by all, but loves no one in return." My voice is monotone, as though I'm reading the side effects of an experimental clinical trial. Healthy individuals who handle Genevieve may experience slight to permanent discomfort. Those that engage in an affair with Genevieve need to proceed with caution and be warned that their heart may not make it out intact. She is not a generic, basic bitch. No insurance policy will cover you.

"You gave her my number? Do you want me or not?" His eyes shift to black. My heart picks up pace like it will burst out of my ribs.

I want him. That was never a question. I'm apprehensive.

Yes, that I am sure. Adrenaline zips through my veins signaling for me to run—I just don't know in which direction. Running towards Hudson and away from Hudson feels truthful. I'm split in half and peg-legging myself in both directions seems the most logical decision made today.

I don't know if he wants me as much as I want him. I'm scared to ask. I momentarily scan the room for a piece of paper to juvenilely scratch out a note that asks him to check *yes* he wants me, or *no* he doesn't. Follow up question if yes, on a scale from one to ten, how bad does he want me? No need for the spoken word. Words only get me in trouble. Let's pass notes back and forth like we did in grade school. Let's dumb us down a bit because I'm out of my league in an accelerated course.

My eyes ping back to his, and his eyes don't pull away. And they don't shift back to gold. He is definitely affected.

"I gave her your number, so you had the option to choose if last night was a haze and this morning was misguided," I say proud of my words and the fact that they came out of my mouth so maturely.

He nods and I sit on the bed. Nauseous, I curl under the covers and lay my head back on the pillow.

"I keep seeing you with her. My brain is working on forgiving and my eyes are etching the image in stone." I hide under the sheets to cover my face. I make a frustrated noise and say, "and I'm scared. I'm scared of what finding you means."

A branch slices against the glass. My eyes won't shed the blackness. The sheets fan out and Hudson slides in behind me. My hands grip the sheet in an iron grasp above my head. He leans over me and we make eye contact in our makeshift tent. His eyes have returned to their golden hue.

"Come here." He reaches for me and pulls me towards him. I unravel and wrap myself around him. My mouth at his ear, I whisper, "Why aren't your eyes black anymore?"

"I don't know," he says.

I don't believe him. "Are you trying to stop your eyes from shifting?"

He rolls us over so he is on his back. "Are you trying to cause my eyes to shift?" His hands corral my hips. I sit up and the left side of my robe slips open off my shoulder. Cold air shocks my skin. Our earlier scene repeats, but there's no skip in the track.

Instantly his eyes blacken and his mouth is on my breast, his tongue scrapes against my nipple.

I press my hands against his shoulders, "Wait, wait..." *Wait, what am I saying?*

His breath blows out across my skin. His hand grasps my robe and lifts it back over my shoulder, "Av?" His voice shudders the flannel like a soft wind under the desert's sun.

In a strange recess of my mind, I know this is a devil's bargain. "This could be dangerous," I say for both his and my sake. He makes me bolder, dirtier, like the criminal I am.

My mind is in a tangle of words hoping I can concoct a brilliant explanation on the whim. I don't, and I begin to scramble and fidget. He pulls me closer until he wraps his lips around my ear and says, "It's just you and me." His hand lowers from the curve of my jaw to wrap around my neck, just beneath my chin, which he keeps upturned. His grasp is loose. I let out a deep breath, feeling grounded and present. We're in the middle of a perfect storm.

He kisses my temple, "Don't leave and hide in the corners of your mind where I can't reach you."

Heavy rain taps a dulcet percussion. He leans back on an elbow—I'm straddling his hips, looking down at him. He's giving me space while beckoning me closer. His black gaze calls to the darkness within me, making every cell sting and cut like tiny needles and blades. I feel every centimeter of my skin. I am every bit alive.

Slowly his fingers slide my robe back off my left shoulder. The fabric gathers again in the crook of my elbow where it seems to fucking belong. I shrug my right shoulder feeling higher than the storm clouds.

I chuck my robe off the bed.

Shooting back up, Hudson grabs and twists us. My breasts are bare to his heated gaze. His lips trail down my body's topography, marking every peak and valley. Like a tourist, he experiences me. His fingerprints embed on my flesh. Each kiss is a dropped pin on his favorite locations. I'm riddled in tiny red flags. Except below the equator, he doesn't visit the southern hemisphere. It's still covered in cotton.

Basking over me, his gaze is like smoke, lingering and soaking into my pores. I shiver, knowing he's the crawling sensation beneath my skin, the vibration in my tremble.

His hand wraps around my ankle and hitches my calf up and over his shoulder. His index finger runs up and down the inside of my thigh.

He kisses the back of my knee and asks, "Do you remember late last night?" His lips don't leave my skin. "You kept tossing and turning." His finger finds three friends that run up and down my hip.

"Your skin was so hot." His knuckles skim against me. "I asked if you were alright." Smirking, he continues, "And you fussed about the heat and tried to push your pants off, but you couldn't work the button. You didn't even open your eyes." His hand leaves my hip and presses down on my lower abdomen where buttons to pants typically rest.

"You helped me take my pants off?" I ask, remembering that I woke up with no pants on. I thought I managed the buttons and shimmied fine in my sleep. *How did I not wake up when his hands touched me?*

A deep purr rumbles out of his chest. "I helped you, but you didn't cool off. You kept getting hotter." His fingers grip my underwear, and he takes on a tortured expression. He drags the thin cloth off my hips and over my ass. He pulls them off my legs and tosses the damp fabric to the ground. "I wanted to take the rest of your clothes off, to have you like this."

Air burns through my lungs. He slips a finger in me and we both moan in pleasure.

I move to reach for him like a flower to the sun. My fingers root in his hair, my teeth nip at the artery at his neck.

He pushes me back down.

The heel of his palm is against my collarbone, his fingers wrap back around my throat. His eyes are at war with himself like he's suffering from a heavy burden, and that burden is me. I'm the weight on his shoulders. I'm the rock in his shoe.

I raise my hands and crisscross my wrists above my head. I shut my eyes.

He slips another finger inside me and curls, calling me closer.

I feel primal insanity like I'm 100% dancing with the devil and my demise is imminent. My death will be tragically sweet, and the ride will be delicious. I lick my lips. My body begging for him. Wantonly craving more.

He pulls his hand out and off of me. My eyes snap open. With a feral expression he says, "Do it again."

Thunder breaks and I look past his shoulder to the rain-blurred windows. The curtains are still open and rain pummels the glass trapping our image within the confines of the room. I speculate what we might look like to any onlooker. Me, naked and thrumming—my leg draped across Hudson's shoulder—arms raised high. He's still fully clothed, dominating. He has me at his mercy.

"Tell me again," he says while running his fingers up and down the inside of my thigh. An invisible trail of cum cools and dries.

"I didn't say anything."

He nods in a way that says he's accepting a challenge.

I nod too. I want whatever he wants. I'll say whatever he wants. Fork the script over, I'll eat it too.

His fingers leave my skin, and he removes my leg from his shoulder. My knees bend and spread.

He's moving in the opposite direction I want him to be in— life in reverse against my will.

"I didn't say anything," I reiterate trying to turn back the hands of time. His hands wrap around my knees and he pushes himself up and off the bed.

"I didn't say anything," not aloud. *Tell me what to say. Come back.*

I release a shuddering breath feeling vulnerable and altogether too naked. I'm like the smoked pig at a banquet, the one you walk by and wonder why'd they leave the head. No one wants to eat piglet. And in the same breath, we're all carnivores —animals tearing another animal's flesh. The realization is unsettling. Just take the head off.

I move to get under the sheets, yet before I can lift the sheet, Hudson says "stay," from across my room. I stop. Time stops. I wait. I stare at the flat white of my ceiling. The once dulcet rain is now heavy-handed like a drum and bass track. Streams overpour from clogged gutters. The icy rain feels inside these walls and coursing through my blood. My skin cools and chills. Again I shiver, but this time Hudson's next to me. His hands tie my wrists against the bedpost with my robe belt. He blindfolds me with my red scarf.

Then he disappears again. My fingers fidget with the excess belt.

I see nothing but blackness. There isn't enough of me remaining to be self-conscious and embarrassed. With my sight gone, my other senses begin to amplify. Sounds are in surround-sound. I can distinguish noises with a finer palate. I'm panting, I sound like a freight train. And I'm trembling in a sea of darkness surrounded by sharks.

The bed shifts and redistributes with Hudson's weight. I sway back and forth on the wave.

A cord brushes against my breast, followed by headphones against my ears. The weight is familiar—he found my pair of noise reduction headphones. All the sounds I categorized previously become a muffled background—muted and refined to white noise.

Music trickles quietly to my ears. Hudson has me connected to his phone. He has me connected to him.

My left headphone lifts, "you good?"

I nod. The restraints and sensory deprivation should make me feel captive, but I feel the opposite. I feel free. I feel safe. My paranoia and neuroses temporarily slip away like a silk ribbon being gently tugged through my fingers. I'm no longer responsible for myself.

The bed shifts again and Hudson leans his weight forward. His breath is like a feather drifting across my skin. My arms jerk instinctively wanting to touch—move closer to relief. My body rocks, but my hands are tethered. Anchored. He has me. I relax back into the restraint.

I'm moaning but I can't hear myself. The volume turns up and music is blaring through my headphones. I'm verbally uninhibited, my words tumble out unchecked and unfiltered. Without warning his mouth goes directly between my legs.

My head knocks back and I scream. I can't hear it. There's a split second where I wonder if I'm as provocative as a porno. Or if I am I shrieking like a banshee. I can't tell, and I no longer care. Because I'm no longer here.

I feel myself leave my body.

Faintly I hear Hudson.

But he doesn't remove the headphones. His mouth is still on me.

I hear him in my mind say, "I hear you begging for me."

Are we fucking telepathic? He chuckles. And it's the sweetest sound I have ever heard. It's over before it started, but it was genuine and it was mine.

I smile and continue to think of all the places I want his tongue. I've heard his voice in my head before but dismissed it. I thought I was delusional. Before it sounded like we were on the same frequency, but the signal was bouncing in and out. It could have been a fantasy.

Now, with my senses deprived, all I can do is tune in and listen to Hudson.

My body releases every type of chemical and thought—dumping endorphins and enkephalins. The release drops me like I've been holding onto hundreds of helium-filled balloons and suddenly Hudson cut the strings.

All at once I drop.

And as I fall, I swear I feel the wind. I feel everything.

The last words I hear are Hudson's velvet purr in the back of my mind, "Fucking give it to me."

7

CHINESE TAKE OUT

THE CLOCK READS wd 00:9. It sits at a precarious position on my nightstand. I'm in bed under the covers. I don't know when I flipped my clock, or even why I would. *Did Hudson flip my clock?* The ludicrously of the question doesn't change the fact— my clock is upside down. And I'm tucked securely in bed. My purple sheets are curled up to my chin.

I search the space next to me for Hudson and am disappointed to find space. Vacant. No visitors next to me. I'm utterly alone.

My eyelids flutter close like the curtains of a play. This is only an intermission. I pretend that I'm not alone—I'm sleeping and Hudson left to go to the bathroom, or he's getting us a snack. He'll be right back. He hasn't left me. There's no need for my heart to be racing the way it is. He'll be just a minute.

I'm not awake.

Everything is okay.

I roll over and a long rectangle of light protrudes beneath my door and hits my eyelids like a lightsaber.

Someone is here. Who is it and why aren't they here *here*, why aren't they close to me?

Frivolous giggling tinkers against the wooden floor. The

sound spreads like glitter during a celebration, shit got everywhere, sank into the miniscule hidey-holes—a constant reminder of previous surface level joys.

Genevieve's laugh reverberates. *What the fuck is so funny?*

I didn't immediately hear another laugh—I didn't hear anything. Genevieve must be on the phone.

I need to take it easy, be a little less twitchy.

But then a man's voice accompanies her laugh. All I hear is the bass. It could be anyone. It could be the television or the radio. I tell myself to calm the fuck down.

Laughing another flirtatious giggle, Genevieve says, "Stop you're making me blush."

An unnerving silence, then, "I tried to call you earlier."

I listen intently to the one-sided conversation—it has too many heart-wrenching pauses. My voice is rejecting words. The only evidence of Hudson and my previous interlude is my scratchy throat.

"What are your plans for tonight?" Her voice is sultry and stifling. The sheets wrapped around me become oppressive. The air gained weight. I need water. My eyes catch on my good ole' unicorn encrusted coffee mug—*how desperate am I?*

"I have a date tonight. I don't have to leave for a few more minutes." Her vowels are provocative. I can imagine her lips forming the words.

The bass responds.

I can't understand what he's saying. His words muffle like he's trying to keep his voice down—keeping the conversation between the two of them—him and Genevieve.

"Let's not talk about her," Genevieve says. Her voice sounds farther away like she's walking from the kitchen back to her bedroom. I barely hear her. "Come over here." The bass never moves. But he responds to her.

Her voice is moving back towards the common area. Back towards the bass. "Don't wait up for me," she says. Her voice is the closest it has been yet. The front door opens. "It was really nice seeing you." She says.

A hushed response, followed by a shut and locked door. The light turns off.

The tension in the air becomes static. *Is Hudson still here?* The possibility of being locked behind a door with him has butterflies fluttering in my stomach. I contemplate waiting for him to come back for me, but my bladder forces my hand.

The crescent moon spotlights me as I get up and walk naked to my dresser. I can still feel Hudson's touch, the strokes of his fingers and the licks of his tongue. My skin feels bruised, even though his touch was soft like he was caressing a bubble. I'm his bubble, and I try to rise higher and higher away from the prick of the needle that threatens to pop my happiness. *Fucking Genevieve.*

I pull out a white nightgown. The silk slips across me; the fabric is smooth like water against river stones.

I open the door to my room.

I don't hear him.

In the darkness, I walk down the hallway with my hands against the walls. The apartment feels haunted.

I turn the corner and instantly feel Hudson's eyes on me. He's behind the glass door on the outdoor patio. One hand is up to his ear. The other is in his pocket. He's unabashedly staring at me while listening to his phone. The technology looks foreign against him. He belongs in the wilderness, away from the city and noise. He's wild. I hate whoever he's on the phone with. I hate whoever is trying to civilize him to society's norms.

His eyes track me. I can't meet his eyes, but I sense his gaze tying my insides into knots and bows.

My gaze is on his body. I look at his clothes and notice he's in a different outfit. Dark jeans and a black shirt. He'd blend into the shadows if it weren't for his golden mane. He's tense like he's ready to pounce.

I make it to Genevieve's room and walk backward through the doorframe. I don't want to turn my back on him. I want to keep looking at him. I want him to keep looking at me. I want him to stop listening to whoever is on the phone with him.

The lock clicks to the full bathroom. I step away from the door. My hand is shaking—fuck he's intense. I'm half expecting Hudson to come crashing through the door like the Hulk or a rabid wolf. I take a deep breath and try to lighten the mood, simmer the vibe. I laugh to myself and think of him crashing through like the Kool-Aid Man from the commercials that aired in the eighties. *Oh yeah.*

I take another step back and come parallel with the mirror. My image reflects eyes wide and bright. I look properly fucked with my hair in disarray, flush and rose-tinted skin—like an ethereal succubus. The dichotomy makes my smile widen.

STEAM FILLS the bathroom and I close my eyes. Memories of this afternoon singe me. They bring potency to the air. I am both powerful and powerless at the same time.

My eyes darken as I recall Hudson's strong hands around my breasts. The sensation of my eyes darkening feels like I'm downshifting and settling into my gears. It's been years since I've been able to drop into this mode and sink into my skin properly.

Heat soaks into my pores.

Rolling my hands along my ribs, I place them in the outlines of where Hudson's hands were earlier. My hands are thinner and much smaller than his. But I want to remember—to feel.

Hot water rushes over my skin, intensifying my fantasy. I pinch my nipple hard at the memory of Hudson's teeth.

My hand slides down my abdomen.

His voice comes at me like a direct hit. "I feel you." He feels behind me, in front of me and inside me all at once. Possessed and invaded, I alter the water to shoot out streams of icicles.

When I step outside the bathroom door, Hudson is waiting for me. His eyes are beaming with pride. "Think of me often?"

I slip past him in my white nightgown. Our bodies touch, but only in a drive-by. I gather and drape my hair over my shoulder and braid the wet strands.

When I look over my shoulder to see if he followed me into the living room—he hasn't. He hasn't moved. I turn fully and walk back toward him.

His eyes are at my throat. With an odd intensity he watches the pounding of my pulse. The right side of my neck is bare and open to him. My hair is heavy on the opposite shoulder. The silk of my nightgown is wet and sticking to my skin beneath my hair's weight.

I call his name and he startles as though I barged into his house and turned on all the lights at once. *Who does that? What did I want?* I'm in his personal space and he's about to push me out.

Yet he doesn't. I'm holding on to him by a thread.

I reach for him and kiss him until he softens. I kiss him to smooth out the snags that threaten to unravel him. I kiss him until he grips me to him and molds us into one against the wall.

His heartbeat battles mine.

Then he pushes away from me; he can only handle me in small doses.

"Fuck," he swears. "I fucking feel you." His black eyes penetrate my mind.

"What do you mean you feel me?" I don't feel him. I only hear him. I don't know how to shut off whatever valve we've opened. It's like I slit my wrist and he's watching me bleed. *Why isn't he bleeding with me? How is our connection not reciprocated?* I cut too deep, and he's not cut at all.

I move to the couch and fold my legs up beneath me. It looks like I'm running away. I might be. *How much access does he have to my mind?*

Hudson joins me a few minutes later with multiple bags that he subsequently unpacks to reveal a Chinese food, wine, and beer. He tells me he didn't know if I drank beer or if I preferred wine. He tells me he got both fried and steamed rice. It looks like he bought the whole left side of the menu. He keeps saying how he didn't know what I liked so he bought ____, but what I hear is—I'm sorry I don't know you and I'm sorry I'm ignoring your question. And instead of answering you, I will explain what's in my bags like a Vanna White magician. He has tricks for me. He has dick for me.

I sit and listen.

Once everything he unpacks is lined out in front of us, I ask again, "What do you mean you feel me?"

He looks down at the food like he wants to go over how many egg rolls he purchased. Why six gets a bad reputation for being unlucky, but in reality, it's the perfect number for egg rolls. The same can't be said for Crab Rangoon. There is a history that he's ready to bullshit on the fly. I just need to hear him out.

I pour myself a glass of wine and look at the multiple little Chinese food boxes. They look like miniature strongholds on my coffee table. Heat wafts from their lids. We're both watching — pretending to be transfixed by the steam.

"You know how there are people who say they see auras?" He asks. I don't respond hoping it's a rhetorical question, and he continues.

He does. "I don't see auras but I sense intentions. Yet with you it's different, I feel your emotions resonate in my blood. You let me in your mind, and I literally feel *in you*." He pauses like he's accepting his truth, saying the words out loud solidifies my effect on him. This is his *'come to Jesus'* moment and I shouldn't trample on them with my atheist's perspective.

"I sense the rest of the world like a nagging jingle stuck on repeat in my head. Earworm white-noise. I can choose to listen or allow it to buzz in the background. With you though..." He stops and shakes his head in reflection. "With you Aviana, I feel your emotions just as well as I feel mine. I feel the surges of your highs, the intense spikes coursing through your body when your eyes go black." He turns toward me. "I feel the toe curls of your orgasm." I can't look at him. My coffee table has never been more interesting.

"You said that being with you could be dangerous, how so?"

I snap my fingers and a single flame flickers from my thumb. I create fire and Hudson doesn't even blink. I see him out of my peripheral vision, he doesn't even move an iota.

Deflated I say, "I have a magic trick; you're supposed to be impressed." I get up and pace the room with my wine. That is the coolest thing I can do. I get the impression I'm not so cool now. The fluttering butterflies in my stomach turn to stone and sink heavy like rocks.

"I've seen you do it before," he says casually as though he didn't just cause an avalanche of change. I stop and stare at him. If he knew, why did he ask? Is he testing me? He acts like he knows nothing about me, but he knows things about me. How much does he know?

"Is it a magic trick or something else?" He questions. I shrug acquiescently. I turn to continue pacing, but before my foot leaves the ground, Hudson has me up against the wall. He moves faster than humanly possible. My mouth is open in a silent scream.

"Something else then?" He asks with his nose up against mine.

"Why do you have so many questions?"

"Because I had no idea you were going to be like this. Because you're the only one I know like me, and you're not even like me. Not really. Just your eyes. But even so, we're so different."

"I don't have any answers, Hudson."

"Tell me about the fire. I've only ever seen you create a flame in the woods to light joints. You were always alone, and it was always with a snap."

"Fuck, why does everything have to be so fucking intense with you." I pause with the need to toss something, break something. Since this isn't really my place, I don't. But the need slithers in my veins. "If I show you mine, you have to show me yours."

He nods, the move looks more like a jerk. I'll take it. I roll my shoulders and slide down the wall until my ass hits the carpet. My knees go up and my chin rests on top of the silk. "Well, if we're going to do this, I might as well introduce myself properly. My name is Lily. But don't call me that."

My arms wrap around my legs. I'm compacting myself as I unpack my many mental boxes. This is the payback for opening my hardcover and letting him into my story.

"If we're going to talk about fire, then we're going to talk about drugs... I fell into the proverbial rabbit hole... Doing drugs gave me the proper setting to play with fire. No one believes a drug addict, and all the ones I met either ended up incarcerated, they overdosed, or they disappeared before anyone riddled out the cause of the arsons... I'm fast too."

WHEN YOU PLAY WITH FIRE YOU GET BURNED

8

LILY WAS ME

TROUBLE TRAVELED FAST, but I traveled faster. I grabbed all the drugs and money I could stash in my bookbag while a fire raged around me.

I was never burned, though I was always *burnt out*.

I sold, smoked, and snorted the stolen product feeling stuck between channels. Constantly grainy and incomplete, like sand left on my skin from the beach. There was always a hair over my shoulder that I could never find. But I felt it, the strand, like a drop during Chinese water torture. *Reminding me, always reminding me.*

TOO BRIGHT FIRES were on my horizon. I was almost there. I could almost catch it.

Just one more hit.

One more, I swear it.

I was too fast, too fast, too fast. I fled from town to town, hopping from one motel room to the next. A string of arsons connected my dots. No point source to the fires. No paper trails. I was invincible as the mobile match—blazing a trail and simultaneously blowing my mind into a dark and twisted depression.

My world was dark.

The dark streets were my friends. Those streets were the devil I knew. We held hands and made pinky promises that we never kept.

MOTEL ROOM FORTY-THREE. I only stayed in rooms with a four or a three, but never duplicated like thirty-three or forty-four.

It made perfect sense.

Rules imposed accountability. I held myself accountable to only staying in certain rooms.

My arsons and other nefarious activities had me consistently letting myself down; therefore, I created random rules as checks and balances. Mass property damage may be my fault, but I kept myself in line. Even if the line was squiggly. I only stayed in certain rooms. If I ever ate anything with my hands, I never ate the section that touched my hands. At the end of a meal, I'd finish with a little handle of a burger or the tail of a hotdog bun that I would later donate to the birds. I held myself to corporate standards, quantity vs. quality—if I did one illicit thing, but followed four or five personal rules, I did more positive than negative. That day was a win. I was a good person.

Inside room forty-three I sat and guzzled down another cold beer. A man with skin the color of dark-roasted coffee sat across from me chopping up pure white lines of cocaine with a driver's license that read Pau Meyers. The letters were printed in bold next to a bald, tattooed photo of the man holding it. The 3D and 2D versions held the same grimace, the same upturn on their right lip.

"I'm doing another hit tonight." My voice was husky from a

virus I was fighting. Probably also due to the cocaine. I blamed the virus.

"Don't rush it, Ana, you went out last night. You're going to draw too much heat." He spoke with authority. Pau was a fugitive who I met at an underground fight. He told me to always bet on crazy, crazy beats tough. Pau was crazy. He'd caress you with the same hand he dragged and beat you with.

But never me, he treated me like his daughter. I was under his care. We scratched each other's itches. Our partnership was beautiful. I searched everyone's pockets while he carried the bulk and cleaned up my impulsive messes.

"That's the point. I'm going to the house on Hickory Ridge." I said waiting for my line of cocaine. I wanted to yell that the line didn't have to be exact. It didn't have to be straight. But I didn't. I waited and waited and waited. Fuck, I waited forever.

"It's a fifteen-minute drive, I'll take you."

"No," I said automatically. Pau always offered to drive me, but I never accepted. He was heavy baggage. He did the carrying. He wasn't created to be fast. I was fast. Pau needed to stay in his lane and stay in the motel room. He didn't know my true skills—he's never seen my eyes.

At midnight, I left.

The night was crisp and the full moon shone like a flashlight. I stepped onto the rickety front porch of the gray house at 9033 Hickory Ridge Lane.

I rocked back and forth, from left to right. The wood creaked and croaked when I shifted like a rocking chair.

A sense of foreboding clung to me like a musty cloak. Most likely from the house number. The house was alive with music. Abandoned, but alive, like a zombie. The bass practically vibrated out of the boarded-up windows. No words, just rhythm.

And then I heard a woman's moan. Porn was pumping throughout the house. Drugs and sex, my favorite combination.

I stretched my arms as wide as they would go and pressed my hands against the wood. My forehead rested against the battered door.

Sparks crackled and popped. Fire grew out of my fingertips and seeped into the wood fibers.

The perimeter of the house caught flame.

I broke down the door.

The fire lurched into the upper level. In a blur, I rushed around shadows stealing their drugs and money like a dark ghost. Strangers ran screaming from their circle jerk.

I was in and out and almost through the window. My reflection was on the windowpane. My fingers nearly on the frame. It was time for me to go.

Then I heard a scream.

I heard a scream that didn't belong to the porn star whose moans still echoed in every room. Her moans sounded like she was choking on cock. The scream I heard was one of pain. A man in pain. A whole new scream, a whole different arsenal of reactions.

Smoke filled the hallways with noxious fumes. The smoke had sticky, gripping fingers. I was still in the little girl's bedroom when I heard the scream for a second time.

I knew that voice.

Pau.

My feet moved in the opposite direction of safety without thought. One moment I was in the princess' room, and in the next, I was in the kitchen by the back door.

Through the fallen debris, I saw him. Pau's crumpled body pinned under a cabinet. His skin was melting. Agonized screams gutted my abdominal cavity as if his voice was an ice cream scooper—his cries carved me. His pleas shredded me—feral and hopeless. It shot straight up my spine and lifted every hair on my body. His pain couldn't be contained and erupted out of him in howls.

He's dead. I was way, way, way too late.

Even with my speed, the distance to the nearest hospital was far, far, away. I ran towards a blue H. Then towards a vibrant, pulsing, red E and R. I was functioning on a basic alphabet skill set.

Tattered and burned, Pau exhaled his last breath in my arms as the automatic doors slid open to the emergency room. *Whoosh.*

I shouted his name, my voice hoarse and gone. He didn't respond. Pau's chest never inhaled. His nostrils didn't expand in a breath. He didn't anything. And I couldn't believe it. I just couldn't believe it.

Strangers in all shapes and sizes stared at me. I only saw them as figures, silhouettes. No faces were prominent between my tears. No words understood. I held Pau tight to my chest. I carried him like he was my fucking princess. His warm blood streamed down my arms and legs, tap-tapping onto the polished linoleum.

I hated everyone's eyes on me. I hated how everyone took more time trying to figure out the mechanics of how a girl that weighed a-buck-ten could carry a two-hundred-pound man. I hated everyone and everything. *Tap, tap, tap.*

No one made a move towards me.

I fell to my knees and released my friend. Medical workers snapped to attention and picked Pau up. They picked up one of *America's Most Wanted* and took him away from me. They took my guy. My arms outstretched towards him, asking without verbally asking for just a second. I need another second with him. This can't be goodbye. He's my guy. *My guy.*

Hands started grabbing me from all angles. I ripped myself away from their clutches and ran. I ran for days. I ran until my legs gave out and I fell in a tumble upon hard branches. I was in the woods, but I didn't know whose. I didn't know where. All I had were my bloodied, torn-up clothes and bookbag full of drugs and loose change.

After a few lines of cocaine, I found myself at a strip joint. Genevieve was a dancer, and I spent almost every penny I stole watching her move. Literal pennies, that's all I had. Her curves were my beacon, and I enjoyed finding myself at her shores. So, I stayed.

She wouldn't come close to me at first. I was still scabbed and tinged with blood—most of it Pau's blood.

I sat in the back corner like the fucking piece of shit that I was, and I gawked at Genevieve like a fucking creeper. I sat through her entire shift. And once she left, I left.

Courtesy of what I stole, I flipped the drugs and bought new clothes and essentials at Wal-Mart. I also found myself a motel within walking distance to the strip joint. I smiled big and bright when I rented room four for the night.

The next night I showed back up at the strip joint looking presentable. I stayed in that cycle, rent a room for one night, shower, sleep & eat, watch Genevieve.

Rent, Rinse, Rest & Restore, Ravage and Repeat.

Once I appeared presentable and pretty, Genevieve liked me. She questioned me a lot. If she wasn't as attractive as she was, I wouldn't have tolerated her. Too many words. Too much maintenance. Always with the, "Why don't you watch anyone else?" or "Why do you do that?"

Repeatedly I told her there was no one else, only her. My heart hurt and was burnt, and she was my milk. I needed a tall glass of her every day. There were no substitutions for how good she made my body feel.

Our interactions were interrogations. Some days her body

said all her words. She'd act more brazen with customers to see my boundary lines.

I wouldn't react because I didn't need to. I only took from her what I needed. And I gave in return my bare minimum. All I needed was to watch Genevieve. The sight of her body washed my fire. Her creamy skin was the aloe to my burns. We didn't have to touch for her to be my antidote. I knew she wanted me, even if she was all up in the jockstrap of married businessmen who cheated on their wives. Regardless, her eyes always returned to me.

One night during a private dance I asked her to coffee, and then to move in with me. I ended up talking my way into her quarters since I was homeless.

She knew my bloodied, dirtied hands. Both our closets were filled with skeletons. I didn't know hers, and she didn't know mine. She never led me to water, only flicked it at my face. We gave each other acceptance and enough sex to get us both on the road to recovery. Or at least perpetuated the illusion, a sparkly mirage.

9

YOUNG LILY'S SHED EXPERIENCE

Technically, I was kidnapped. But I didn't consider myself kidnapped. My captor didn't have any intention of returning me. He wasn't holding me for ransom. No one searched for me.

They stole my time—I was fucking stolen.

In my childhood room, my twin bed had matching night-stands on either end. The window was open, songbirds were singing. The day was glorious and radiating innocence.

Until a heavy presence likened to marmalade poured down my back. I felt transparent, the ooey-gooey flowed through me. The presence was tangible, yet I didn't see it. Paralyzed with fear that a ghost was about to prove all my nightmares true, I held my breath and cried silent tears. My mouth made the form to yell out for my mom. My voice choked and only creaked a plea, *"mommy"*.

Slowly the heaviness condensed into a dark human shape, as if it materialized only to balance me mentally. I was only a kid. I firmly believed the boogeyman found me. I knew he lived in the closet and had a timeshare with the creepy crawlers from under my bed. Like a cockroach, the boogeyman stuck to dark-ness, he was nocturnal. *What was the boogeyman doing in the light of day?*

The human form sludged closer to me and tossed an icky version of fairy dust on me that caused me to sleep. Not only sleep, but to be comatose.

When I roused, I awakened to dark wood walls. There was a ceramic tub and two buckets. Neither bucket had labels, only one was filled with water. It took me pissing my pants a few times to realize what the second bucket was to be used for. There were no windows, only one naked bulb attached to the ceiling that never turned off.

The dark form became all I knew. My savior and abductor. The being formed and dissipated at random, and when it formed it overwhelmed and suffocated the small shed. The only consistency I knew was an injection every day. The side effects were intense drowsiness. While I slept my adolescence away, my shed was cleaned, food was deposited and a fresh bar of soap was left on top of a nicely folded towel. Of the three happenings that occurred while I slept, the folded towel irked me the most. The corners were ironed.

My only friends were imaginary. Spiders didn't venture between the slits of the dark wood panels. Only a slight draft from heavily winded days breached my shed. My imaginary chatterbox friends constantly prattled me with, "Lily, be silent. You may learn something new if you listen. You talk too much. All you're doing is repeating what you already know. And you know nothing silly child," and "Lily, never make a decision when you're sad. And for heaven's sake don't reply when you're angry. When you are happy, do not ever make a promise. However, Lily girl, you're never happy here." Or the ever prominent, "Lily, everything that you are going through is preparing you for what you asked for."

Yet I didn't ask for this.

"Lily girl, when one door closes a window, door, or any alternate exit path opens and widens its welcoming arms. Stay open." They said.

My friends also preached that I'm responsible for the effort and not the outcome.

And it's not that I stopped caring, I simply stopped caring about things that needed to be forced to work. I couldn't force the door open, so I stopped looking at it. I couldn't rationalize with my imaginary friends, so I let silence do my talking. At a mental precipice, I became numb. Then my friends ticked me off, and I became indifferent.

On what I later found out to be my twelfth birthday, I felt my first spark—an electric shock went through my entire being. I seized and shook like a wet dog. Flames flew off me like water droplets. I lost consciousness and woke up in the ceramic tub with the shed burned down. It wasn't unusual for me to be waking up in the tub since it doubled as my bed. It was unusual that everything else surrounding the tub was black and ash.

I jumped out of the tub and ran off the premises as fast as my little feet could go—which was a lot faster than expected. Or what it should have been with my muscle atrophy.

I REEKED TO HIGH HEAVEN, but I snuck into the gala, anyway. There were masses of over-jeweled women with pompously tailored men. Within the thick of the crowd stood my mother and father. I wanted my mommy.

One of the catering staff saw me as I was about to enter the crowd. They pulled me aside and spoke to me like I was seven, which was fine since I was mentally stagnant around that age. Bodily, I was all lanky limbs and chewed nails. I waited on the front lawn, buzzing and full of childish energy. It felt like the night before Christmas and all through the house merriment spread. I was finally coming home. The staff lady was bringing my parents.

I saw them turn the corner and their eyes weren't bright

with light, no cheery welcome in sight. My parents came with an uproar of displeasure.

I reached towards her instinctively and she pulled back—my dirty fingers inches from her light gray sheath dress.

All the color drained from my mom's face. Her pallor matched her dress. I tried to apologize and explain that I was Lily Williams, that I was her daughter. No one believed me; they only saw the dirt and grime and said, "No not here, not right now." To my ears, it was more "NO, FOR GOD'S SAKE NO! NOT HERE! NOT RIGHT NOW!" This world I rushed back to was harshly loud. Everyone's mouth connected to a loudspeaker. No one used an indoor voice.

They took me to a hotel, room twenty-two. Roughly they chucked me into another tub and told to clean myself. To my ears, I was abrasively screamed at—verbally assaulted by the barrage of voices. Lab technicians and phlebotomists came and took oral swabs and my blood. Policemen hovered by the door. There were too many black suits. I kept thinking, *not another black suit*. But they infiltrated like ants. I was a security risk. Lab coats and badges invaded my personal space and swarmed in mass. My parents were absent amongst the chaos, deciding to wait out the torrent of professionals in the adjoining room. My parents wouldn't take ownership of me, not unless our DNA matched. They continually reiterated DNA, DNA, DNA. I continually questioned what D had to do with N, and why was A at the end? This wasn't the alphabet I recognized.

The scientists said my DNA was altered. They stared at me, they held up reports and stated phrases like, 'off the charts' and my favorite, 'she's abnormal'.

At first, there was a lot of 'something must be wrong' statements. Once my specimens were tested and then repeated for confirmation, the science was irrefutable. Computers didn't lie, humans did. I did, *but I didn't*.

I traded one captivity for another. I wasn't allowed to move without being monitored and asking for permission beforehand. No one touched me unless they stole from me. My fluids. My blood. My time. I bled just the same as anyone else. I didn't understand. I couldn't talk back.

What bothered me most was the loss of time. I had no perception. Months turned into a mystery number. I lost count of how many sleeps I had. The maturing of my body marked time. I had boobs, and no one bought me a training bra. Light blue scrubs were all I wore. As a result, when I bled through my light-colored scrubs I learned I wasn't dying but in fact menstruating.

In a room full of people, I learned about the 'birds and the bees' from Times Roman words. I kept wearing the light blue scrubs, even when they laid out darker colored scrubs for me to wear instead. I took a sick pleasure in the disturbed glances I received from my bloodstained pants. I wanted them uncomfortable.

Mostly, I kept silent and people started to trickle away. I never saw my parents again. As a rule, no one left me alone; I was still a subject of scientific discovery. One guard, one me, seemed simple enough.

Except one night I was sleeping one moment and grabbed the next. My head whipped against the cement. Lights out.

I came to in the middle of a black burn circle. A charred body lay next to me. That was the first time I was aware I killed someone.

Later I deduced he was most likely trying to rape me and the fire within me ignited as a survival mechanism. Rape was a concept I learned from a stack of brochures they left me. One of them was about domestic violence and assault. With as much monitoring as I had, no one reviewed my reading material. The phlebotomists and guards grabbed whatever was handy to throw at me for entertainment: maps, brochures, pamphlets, the Bible, and menus. A few raggedy magazines rounded out my reading materials.

Once again, my world was too silent. Though this time in the positive sense. I lay in the black circle of death and heard no fire alarms. No safety came. No one else was in the building. I sprang up, got out, and got to running.

I found myself at the doorstep of the only home I knew. I was alone on the property. I ran up to my room and grabbed jewelry and anything that looked expensive. My room was a time capsule on its way to being a guest room. Unfolded boxes leaned against the wall. They binned my clothes up, ready for donation.

I snatched the emergency cash stash from my father's office drawer. By the backdoor, I skimmed through a stack of mail. It was right there by the bananas, I heard my father open the front door. My eyes were on the envelopes with four bananas as the backdrop. Yellow, like the caution of a streetlight. I paused. *Would I make it before everything turned red?*

I bolted.

I clutched the mail to my chest and hid in the pantry. I heard the clip of my father's fancy shoes get closer. He was on the phone—he kept saying he was late to see Grace; he was late for visitation hours. Late to see my mother. He stomped around a bit more and left back out the front door.

In my scurry to hide, I dropped an envelope. The top was fringed and haggard. I opened the shredded jaw and pulled out its white tongue of information. I held a bill for a psychiatric ward. My father had my mother institutionalized.

I ran because that's what children do. I ran and inherently believed everything was my fault. It was my fault they stole me. It was my fault my mother had a mental break from the burden of my reappearance. I deserved the life of crime I turned to. I deserved nothing but crumbs. I was nothing but trouble.

FROM HIS VOICE I MAY BE DEAD

THE READING CORNER

HUDSON

My mother named me after the Hudson River. She lived in a small historic river town that we never visited. When I asked her where my namesake came from, she said very matter of fact, "I missed the bus and had to walk a long way home. Your grandfather would whip me for missing dinner. That night he chased me off onto the frozen river. His weight sent him through the ice. When I was a child, I thought the river that swallowed him was the Hudson River." It turned out not to be the Hudson River, but the name was already associated with the memory.

Wisconsin was where I grew up. A quaint town whose football team was their shining glory and their seasonal fairs were the talk. Raised by parents Mary and Christopher Thomas, both were respectable mathematics teachers at the local high school. I have a much older brother named Christopher Kevin, who we called Kevin. As the first-born son, Kevin received the patriarchal name. Since I'm the backup son, I received whatever my mother chose.

With a twenty-two-year age difference, neither my brother

nor myself were planned pregnancies. Other than my accidental birth, my life was regular and obnoxiously normal.

On a typical night in suburbia, I rounded the corner to
Terra's house. We lived in the same houses our whole lives.
Kicked rocks and picked up sticks together.

Within ten minutes, I'm at her doorstep. I allowed myself
entrance without knocking. "Terra!" I hollered. My voice echoed
in the one-story blue house.

"Be there in a minute."

I sat down in my regular spot on the brown frumpy couch
and occupied myself talking to the family basset hound, Earl.
He had big floppy ears, wrinkles on wrinkles, and large droopy
eyes—the Eeyore of dogs. I scratched behind his ears and he
looked at me with a stoned, appreciative expression. He acted
like he hadn't been loved on in a while and that bothered me.
How a person treats their pet is telling of how they treat others.
We're all animals with different sets of limitations.

"I was quick, see, only a minute," Terra said as she walked
down the hallway. I looked down at my watch and listened to
her melodic voice get closer. I counted fifteen minutes.

Black hung onto her every curve in a criminal appeal. My
mouth glued shut as if I just jabbed a spoonful of peanut butter
on my tongue. My math skills instantly lost credibility: $1+1=$
Terra.

"Ready to go?"

"Waiting for you." I teased. I stood up and hugged her. Four
inches shorter than me at 5'8, her head rested snug on my
shoulder.

Every guy in town chased her. She was oblivious and placed
everyone in the friend zone. There were no other zone options.

I've seen her though, and I've heard her melodic voice in
dark corners where no songbird should be singing. She could
never be invisible. Not to me.

"Well, then let's go." She pulled my hand into hers and laced our fingers together. I looked down at our clasped hands and smiled. We instinctively held hands. Maybe it was a reflex. The blame should be on our mothers, our friend's mothers, and the women who believed they could be a better mother than our own, though they never had children. Those were the women who constantly scolded anyone knee level and below to hold each other's hand. Use the buddy system. Scream fire in danger and always look both ways.

The reality was that I held Terra's hand because I wanted to. I held her hand because it felt right. I reached for her. I reeled her in. I didn't know if Terra felt the same. For as much as we talked, our communication was sorely lacking.

Too old for trick-or-treating, but never too old for ghost stories, we were on the hunt. The closest reported haunted location beside a cemetery was the local bookstore, *The Reading Corner*, which closed just before dark.

We had the streets to ourselves. At night, demons came out to play. In the dark, the air was intimate and traitorous. It tasted sweet on the tongue, like a poisoned caramel apple.

The Reading Corner was a small narrow shop at the end of Parson St. It seamlessly connected to the flower shop, *Tulips for You*, which had a dozen small wind chimes at the shop's entrance.

Our steps dropped off the sidewalk to the street. *The Reading Corner* was a block away. We could hear the soft harmonious song of the wind tinkering off the chimes. A full moon bathed us in an ominous light. The ambiance added to the ghost stories I told Terra as we walked. I spoke quietly so she would have to lean into me. The stories were of over-dramatized employee experiences. Books grew legs and moved, cabinets flew open, water and lights switched on and off. *The Reading Corner* was infamous for ghosts running through bookshelves and tossing books in the aisles.

After a ten-minute walk, we reached *The Reading Corner's*

back door. Terra used to volunteer part-time—she sideswiped and copied a key.

My hand was dropped like a bad habit. Terra clawed through the black hole of her purse for the copied key.

The key slipped in the lock and the door creaked open. Terra walked in first and I followed. She crept into the center aisle and sat down rummaging in her massive purse.

If any otherworldly sightings would come out and play, we would see it. We were center stage.

Sitting down beside her I asked, "What have you there?"

"One of us has to come prepared." Terra pulled out a blanket, and a thermos filled with hot chocolate. Taking the initiative, I flapped out the blanket and laid down on my back. Terra lied down next to me. Only our arms touched. Her baggage sat tipped against the cashier station.

"So do you think we're going to see something?" She asked the ceiling.

"I don't know T."

"You never believe." She gave me a shove, sat up, and drank hot chocolate.

We sat and laid down. Then laid down and sat for hours. Nothing changed besides the conversation topics. Every few minutes—or if there was a lag in the conversation and silence settled on us—Terra would claim she heard a book fall.

Her posture corrected to search the surroundings. "Did you hear that?"

I didn't hear shit, but I got up on cue and walked the aisles. Terra stepped on the backs of my shoes until we confirmed no dropped book and no ghost.

Back to our blanket, we got back to sitting. We ran out of hot chocolate and memories. Our nostalgia drained, which left melancholy current events.

Terra smiled up at me, and I smiled down at her in return.

Silence hugged us both until she asked, "So, are you and Jenny a thing?"

She lied down after her question. Flat on her back, she looked up to the ceiling as though it was transparent and she could navigate the constellations. I laughed and lied down on my side, "She wants to be." What I wanted to see was beside me. I wanted to navigate the narrow path of Terra's thoughts, the open stream of her dreams. She turned towards me like a restless sleeper, rolling her thoughts around as if it were a piece of hard candy. "Have you done anything with her?"

Terra's doe-like eyes left her vulnerable. We never talked about each other's flings. When we were together, it was just us. Now it seemed like she wanted to bring in every Kelly, Debbie and now Jenny I'd ever talked to.

"We went to a few football games."

"I meant have you done-done anything with her?" She asked over my shoulder to the countless shelves that surrounded us.

"Yeah, sure, we've been spending time together. What about you and Bryan?"

Her bold, innocent eyes turned back to mine. "Bryan, what about Bryan?"

"I saw you last Friday sneaking under the bleachers with him. What have you been up to?"

"Nothing, I mean he tried, but I don't like him."

"So who do you like? You could have anyone in town."

"Did you hear that?" She asked in her signature meerkat stance—her back straight and head on a swivel.

I hadn't heard a sound. Regardless we made the rounds.

"Are we going to stay until sunrise?" I asked while my free hand skimmed across biographies. We turned into the War, History and Politics aisle.

"If you want to, we haven't seen anything yet. I think we will if we stay."

"Sure we will."

"Now you believe?" She pushed me lightly. I over-dramatized my fall and slid down foreign language and travel books. Hands on her hips she waited for me. Her eyes scanned the books on the top two shelves. She pulled one down and tossed it at me. *Castles in the United States* fell into my lap. The Oheka Castle on the front cover.

"No, I just don't want to go home." My cookie-cutter house was cold—a broken home with a pristine exterior and a white picket fence. Terra was my sanctuary. She was my true home; the place I slept was just walls and a roof. I reached up to her. Our hands clasped, and I pulled myself up. The Oheka Castle stayed grounded.

We were headed from gardening to cooking when she said, "You know people still ask me if we're dating."

My elbow nudged her. "By people do you mean Jenny? I know you guys are close."

"She's in my ear all day and night asking questions, then if I don't tell her what she wants to hear explicitly she gets whiny and high pitched. I could just punch her in the face."

"What does she ask you?"

"Her favorite question is whether you talk about her to me. And since you don't, it is also what enrages her the most. She tries to convince me you love her and I try to support her fantasy. But I just want to punch her in the face, like she's a whack-a-mole."

I laughed at her fiery tone, "I'm sorry T." My apology didn't seem very convincing with my smile spread cleanly across my face, "I had no idea what she and I were doing was filtering down to you, and the damage... the damage it was causing to you... I'll stop seeing her."

"If you really like her..." But before she could finish her thought, I finished it for her, "I don't. I'll say something to her tomorrow."

"Really?" Her eyes gleamed in a way that I'd never noticed before.

"Really T, you know you're the only girl I can actually tolerate."

Terra fidgeted with the perfect vegan diet books on the shelves. I could practically see her blend and mix reasons on why I spent time with her. None of which showed a preference to her, rather a kinship to the proximity of our houses. Every other house around us stored children too young or too old.

"When Jenny wasn't assaulting me with questions, she was telling me stories... of you guys... in detail."

"Did she make you uncomfortable?"

"She did." Terra turned and walked back to the blanket. I gave her a minute before returning. I sat down next to her and placed my hand on her knee. My mouth opened to apologize when she started, "She did make me uncomfortable... But I was uncomfortable because I was jealous. I want to know what it feels like." My hand slipped off her knee and slid up her thigh. It may have been a Freudian slip. It may have been intentional. Either way, I was closer to the motherland. "You want me to show you?"

"I don't know." She whispered.

"T, I won't think any differently of you if you don't want to."

"It's not that I don't want to-"

It's that she didn't know what to do. And she wasn't sure if she could pull off appearing sexy. Her innocence was practically wafting off of her in great plumes that would nauseate some and attract others.

"Did you hear that?" I asked even though I had heard nothing, but I knew how flighty she was and I didn't want her to think she fell into a hole that she couldn't get out of. Terra startled and jumped up looking around.

I grabbed her hand, and we searched the grounds again. She dawdled through the aisles and I walked beside and slightly behind her. Normally I led. This rotation I pressed her forward. She seemed frightful and nervous, but at least she was out of her head.

"Where did you hear the noise?"

"In the back," I whispered close to her ear. The back of the bookstore was shadowed off from windows. It was the section of the bookstore she feared most. The horror, crime, and mystery novels were shelved in the dark corner.

"How sure are you that there was a noise back there?"

"Very sure."

Her steps inched closer without lifting off the carpet until she reached the corner. I peered over her shoulder and saw her scrunched face and eyes sealed tight. I pulled a book down off the shelves and it smashed against the floor beside her feet with a heavy thud. She screamed and turned around and hid in my shoulder while I laughed, "I told you I heard a noise down here."

She punched me.

"You're such a jerk!" She pounded her small mighty fists against my chest on the verge of tears.

I wrapped my arms around her and held her tight. "I'm sorry, you're such an easy target, I couldn't resist." Each breath of my words fluttered her short hair.

"Can I have my hands back?" Terra asked into my chest.

"Are you going to play nice?"

"Are you?"

"Always T." I loosened my hold—her hands slipped down to her sides. I leaned into her and kissed her. Our first kiss happened with a fondness and tenderness of a kid's kiss on a dare. My lips touched hers and she didn't kiss me back. She did nothing. Then I did nothing. Awkwardness filled and expanded the air between us like a balloon about to pop.

Then her lips parted, and she went up on tiptoes to kiss me sweetly. Her leg should have kicked back and I should have dipped her. We were in a moment that I ruined. My hands didn't dip; instead, they pulled on her curves. I pressed her into the bookshelf.

Our kissing began to intensify; our petting became groping. Hastily she unzipped my sweatshirt and pulled it off me. The removal of my clothing felt almost clinical.

I couldn't figure out how to remove her sweater. It had giant fucking buttons that crossed her asymmetrically. By the time I figured it out, the moment was almost tarnished again. I defeated the sweater and was rewarded with a black lace bra.

"Babe, you're so beautiful." I pressed my mouth against her neck and then slipped lower to kiss her cleavage. As I unstrapped her bra, I caught the weight of her breasts with my hands and pressed my face between them. My lips trailed down her stomach until I unbuttoned her black jeans and pulled them down with her black lace panties. On my knees, I pulled out both her legs from under her and caught her as she fell onto my lap.

My chest was about to cave in. Hopefully, my spontaneity and the darkness was keeping her out of her head. I don't think she's ever been naked in front of a guy. I don't know, maybe I should have asked. I had too many questions, too many sensations ambushing me. I kissed her until I forgot my name.

With her legs wrapped around me, she started to grind against me.

"Are you sure about this?" I asked as I unbuckled my pants.

She nodded into my neck and I couldn't contain myself further. I snatched a condom from my wallet in my back pocket. I've never been so happy that I kept a condom in my wallet for 'just in case'.

Slowly, she eased on me.

"Am I hurting you?"

She shook her head and moaned a response I couldn't interpret.

THAT NIGHT as I walked Terra home, the sunrise behind us, everything felt right. I stopped us at almost every tree and pressed her back against the rough bark. I kissed her and held her. Physically I couldn't get enough of her touch. Her taste was too fleeting. Her warmth was never close enough.

She said she gave me her virginity. I couldn't shake the impression that I took it. I stole it like a thief.

That night, that blissful night, I promised her I would keep her safe. I promised her that everything would be ok. I held her tight. I held her like she was mine. Because she was. Everything felt right.

MY HOME

HUDSON

Days and weeks fell off the calendar and puddled into months. Terra and I cocooned ourselves with each other.

Together we were isolated.
We were an island.

In the dark of night, I tapped on Terra's window and spent a brief few hours with her warm in my arms. At dawn, I'd wake and crawl out the same window to meet her at the front door to walk her to work. We were both in the in-between of life, stuck between the pauses of graduating and succeeding as adults. We worked odd jobs to make little money. We were lost in the chaos of choices that life handed out. We debated all the options. All the collars I buttoned around my neck were strangling, whether blue or white.

My life was a roaring failure. But Terra was all that mattered. She was it. She radiated brighter than any star or sun in the sky when I was near. Her smile filled my heart and brimmed over to satiate my soul.

I wouldn't break her. The thought of letting her down made me physically nauseous. She would always be young and innocent to me. I didn't want her to believe she made a mistake. For me to be that mistake. I couldn't risk losing her. Not now. Not ever.

I understood our relationship was a marathon and not a race. I'd run until my ankles hurt. And I did, for a year.

ON OUR ONE-YEAR anniversary from *The Reading Corner*, I had an extra pep in my step. The damp wind rustled through my hair when I left the local jewelers. In my front pocket was my most recent purchase, a silver diamond-encrusted heart pendant necklace. I was a hopeless romantic filled with clichés and swooning gestures. It was in this euphoric daze that I crossed the street lazily walking in between the boundaries of the pedestrian crosswalk. I was warmer than warm. And it was within this flurry of emotions that I didn't notice the car accelerating towards me. A silver rusted excuse for a vehicle pressed the gas with a heavy foot. I didn't have the time to blink, let alone move.

BEEP... Beep... Beep...

I TRIED to move my arms, but I came across a resistance. I should be standing on the street. *Why wasn't I on the street?* My eyes burned as I tried to open them. It took time for my eyelids to separate and even longer for my vision to focus. Cream walls with a sterile scent surrounded me. Weathered brown leather straps restrained me. The beeping increased as fear surged through my veins. I shot up breaking my restraints and ripped out all the needles from my arms. The beeping flat-lined. I snuck out of my hospital room without a second thought. Too much fear and pain bombarded me. I just wanted to be home. *My home.*

I ran straight to Terra's house. My ass in full moon because of the hospital gown.

I took a few deep breaths before I tapped lightly on the window. It took a few minutes of incessant tapping before the window opened.

Terra grabbed me and pulled me close to her crying, "Hudson... How are you here?" Her hands pressed against my face—touching me to verify my reality—my three-dimensional shape was in question. *Wasn't I just on the street?*

Moonlight was the only source of light. A ray pierced through the window and lit Terra's neck at just the right angle that sent off a flash. I pulled the spark from around her neck and held the heart pendant in my hand, "You're wearing the necklace I bought you."

She flushed a deep red that I missed and I kissed her. My kiss was short since her tears streamed laces down her face.

"Everything is alright babe, calm down," I whisper to her, holding her close against my chest.

"How... How are... How are you here?"

At her question, I took the second I hadn't taken yet. *How did I get here? How did I break the restraints? Why was I at the hospital? Why did my eyes burn? How am I not winded or injured?*

I had no answers.

"I woke up in the hospital scared and all I wanted was to be home, and you're my home, Terra. You're my home."

"This doesn't make any sense."

"Which part?"

"You were in a hit-and-run accident. You had severe injuries and have been in a coma for almost five months. It's been nineteen weeks and four days."

"No... I was just on the street-"

"The doctors had hope for you. No one gave up hope that you would wake up. The medical team didn't understand why, but you would have extreme night terrors and they had to put you in restraints."

"-no, please Terra stop talking." I separated myself from her and opened the window wider for air. Claustrophobic, we may have only been whispering to each other, but it sounded as if she was yelling at me. COMA? NIGHT TERRORS? FIVE MONTHS?

"I'm just trying to help fill in the blanks."

My voice suddenly filled with sorrow, "Just because I don't remember, doesn't mean that I want to."

"You shouldn't be able to walk. You shouldn't be here right now. What if something happens? I'm not capable of taking care of you."

We were both tormented, her with confusion and me with hurt.

"What do you think I'm going to do?" I asked with my arms spread. I wore only a hospital gown; my ass was literally in the breeze.

She turned away and whispered to the wall, she couldn't face me. "I don't know Hudson, that's what I'm scared of."

"I'm sorry, I didn't mean to scare you."

REALITY HAD A VERY BITTER TASTE. It was toxic and venomous and carried no warning labels.

My feet led me to my family's house, and I slipped my dirty feet under the covers of my cold bed where I closed my burning eyes. I couldn't sleep. Mary, my mother, came into my room when the sun was still rising in the sky and screamed. Someone pulled her out of the bedroom and shut the door.

All I saw was the ceiling, life happened in my peripheral. When I closed my eyes, life ceased to happen. Sleep was like death, a death that didn't torment my family. I was dead to the world, yet still breathing.

Later the door opened again and a flood of medical professionals entered and tried to poke and prod me. I refused any treatment. I was furious and scared and just wanted to be alone in my misery. The sun descended as a stream of family and friends entered and left. I remained silent and still. There was too much noise. Far too many voices. None of them the one I wanted to hear until the door opened again late at night.

"Hudson..." Terra's sweet voice filled my room. I took a deep watery breath at her presence.

"Your family's worried about you." She said moving closer to me. I still wouldn't look at her. I hadn't looked at anyone.

My family was worried. I understood that from earlier. It still didn't explain why she was here.

"What do you want?" I sounded colder than I expected.

"I told you, your family is worried, and they asked if I could help to see if you were okay."

"I'm fine," I said between grinding teeth. Because isn't that what we always say when we're *not* okay. *I'm fine.* Everything is okay.

"Why don't you let the doctors do their examinations?"

"I'm fine." I felt stronger and faster than I ever felt before physically, but mentally I was shattered.

"You're not fine Hudson."

"What do you want?"

"I told you..."

I interrupted her, "You told me what my parents told you to say, what are you doing here? Last night I scared you and now you're here trying to fix me. You're what broke me, Terra. So I'll ask you again, what are you doing here?"

She didn't know what to say, so she lifted the covers and crawled into my bed. Against my own determined will, I rolled to my back and pulled her to me.

"I love you... you're my home and the thought... the thought that I frighten you. I'm completely out of control... I mean how has it been almost five months when everything feels the same?"

She looked at me like she had prepared for me to be crippled or handicapped. She hadn't prepared for me to be *normal*.

Her hands traced my face and I closed my eyes and listened. She told me what she did while I was in a coma which entailed a lot of sitting by my side doing crossword puzzles. She reacquainted herself with my responsive self and my dick felt the separation from her fingers more than anything. She kissed my eyelids, and I opened them with nefarious thoughts in mind.

We made eye contact.

And she screamed bloody murder.

Her scream pierced my ears and scratched deep in my brain. Her love coursed over my skin one-second, then was replaced by a firehose spray of ice. The pressure and flip were too intense.

I reached for her and she backed away screaming louder. I didn't think she could get louder, but she proved me wrong. She also proved that her fear derived from me.

I was her fear.

I would never forget the sheer terror in her eyes when she looked directly into mine. I was the perceived threat that she was trying to escape and I collapsed at the thought. I discontinued existence.

My parents barged in with worry stricken faces and Terra ran out of my room in hysterics. My poor parents looked back and forth, unsure which person needed the most immediate attention first. Who was bleeding out the fastest? Not me, I already bled out. I made the decision easy. Don't fight for me.

Terra slipped through my fingers. The harder I fought for her, the farther and faster she ran. *What the fuck happened?*

THE FIRST TIME I saw my eyes reflected at me in the mirror I noticed they were yellow. My light brown eyes had somehow altered to piercing wolf eyes. Eyebrows raised I stood motionless. All the air knocked out of my ribs. I shook violently—I almost fell to the ground again like a damsel in distress. I gripped onto my dresser. My hands clutched tight.

I clenched my eyes tighter. I felt fine, everything fucking good and gravy. I have brown eyes. My eyes are the color of shit. My eyes are shit.

All my suppressed stress pressed deep into the dark wood of my dresser—I clung for support. I opened my eyes and ripped out chunks—my eyes were no longer yellow but black. It was as if my pupils enlarged and swathed my eyes entirely in darkness. No wonder Terra was terrified, I looked demonic, and I passed out at the thought.

It was light outside when I came to with my face flat on the ground, head rocking. I got to my feet and ran out of my house like it was on fire, or I was on fire.

I found myself at Terra's front door. My feet always tried to send my ass home. I knocked loudly on the door and waited for Terra to answer. I would have gone to her window, but I didn't want to startle her any more than I already had. The door swung open and my heart sank, it was her father. He was a very large, demeaning, grizzly looking man. "What in tarnations are you doing son?"

"Is Terra in?" I asked and peered around the massive man. I couldn't see her. The man was barrel-chested, all I saw was the wall. It was a neutral color, probably called pecan or cappuccino. Or maybe something less appetizing but aesthetically pleasing like sandcastle brown. All I saw was a prison, walls, and barriers that held me back, barriers that held Terra away.

"She's sleeping, it's five in the morning."

"Right... I'm sorry I bothered you." I turned to leave with sunken shoulders.

"My daughter came home last night crying her eyes out."

My feet stopped, and I shook slightly in anguished shame. *Fuck me sideways.*

"I never fought with her for having a boy for a best friend, but you never made her cry. You're supposed to protect her. We've had this conversation before son." Indeed, we had. The conversation happened when I was ten and I had taken great pride in my promise to protect Terra. The boys in our class had been teasing Terra for her gangly limbs and too tall stature. Her father spoke to me about it, made me promise to watch out for her physical safety, and later the safety of her heart. The next day I was suspended for giving the bullies each a black eye. I wasn't sorry. Terra's father ended up taking us for ice cream and giving me a high-five.

"Sir..." I turned around to defend myself. But before I could get out the words, Terra's father had his own to share, "Are you on drugs son?"

"No, sir-"

"Do you take me for an idiot? What drugs are you taking?"

"No sir, I do not and am not. I had an adverse reaction in the hospital- "

"I trusted you with my daughter!"

"Sir, I'm not on drugs-"

"I'm looking straight in your eyes! Get off my property!"

The door slammed. I was torn between trying to reach Terra and leaving her behind. I wasn't meant to be from a broken home. This felt like an unamicable divorce.

Before I could make the decision, her father opened the door again with a shotgun aimed straight for my blackened eyes. The choice was made for me.

I ran.

Once my legs started pumping, I disappeared at a speed that exceeded human capabilities. I sensed the currents of the wind change as a bullet whizzed by my face. Almost instantly I was off their property. I took refuge behind the trees in the wood-line around their house and watched Terra's maniac father search for me.

The sound of the gunshots brought Terra out of the house in her pajamas, she wasn't wearing the necklace. Her father stopped shooting at figures he believed were me and turned to his only child.

"That boy had the nerve to come by and see you!" Her father shouted. Terra paled, her ghostly complexion emphasized her swollen eyes and dark circles.

"Don't worry honey he's gone. I don't think he'll be coming back either." Her father's words seemed to console her. They fucking brought her peace. Her expression lifted and she even let out a sigh of relief.

I sank to the ground with a crushed soul.

I lost her.

I was officially homeless.

"Why don't I take you out for breakfast?" Her father asked. Terra gave a small sheepish smile and went inside to change. A few minutes later, they left.

I didn't.

I sat there for a better part of an hour before I made a resolve to break into their house and into Terra's room. I found the pendant necklace in the trash. I picked it up with shaky fingers and slipped it in my front pocket.

12

WANDERLUST

HUDSON

My small town in Wisconsin became an even smaller town in my rearview mirror. Windows down, music blasting, I screamed until all my words dried out. I was homeless, I might as well get stuck in a wanderlust. I had nowhere to be and nothing to do.

From town to town I picked up odd jobs and lived in run-down motel rooms and on coworker's couches. Some nights I pulled over on country roads and slept in the cab. I didn't sleep much; it was more like I blacked out for a period. A forced reset.

I ambled through life in a cold manner. I was hostile and exceedingly rude. If I could shed my skin like a snake and leave myself, I would. Everything about me was toxic.

My cell phone stayed turned off and fully charged. I only kept it for emergencies. Every few days on a wasted lonely night I turned it on and listened to old missed voice messages. I never returned a call. No one heard back from me at my earliest convenience.

I didn't have a customized voicemail. It was the robotic message that read my phone number back. My callers didn't reach a human. I no longer felt human, I was 1-534-266-... And I am unavailable.

Throughout the first 24 hours, my phone blew up; and then blew less like the whistler grew weary and stopped making noise. Everyone stopped calling. My parents stuck around the longest, but eventually, they too stopped. Their last message went, "Hudson, this is your father calling again. I can only assume that you're ok. Come home, or call if you want. You know how to reach us. The door is always open. Take care son." Click. Message received.

Terra never called.

Only when I was truly wasted, I unleashed the hounds and listened to her singsong voice from saved old voice messages. With my eyes closed and the speaker next to my ear, her words chewed me raw. They ripped me apart and called me to her in the same phrase. She was right next to me.

I'd listen to her tell me she was on her way back from work. She was excited to see me. Could I stop by? Could I bring a bottle of wine? Maybe pick up dinner. She was thinking something Italian.

Her voice messages were mainly random reminders and updates.

Honestly, it didn't matter what she said. What I heard was she missed me. I was on her mind and she wanted me to know she was safe. She wanted to see me. But most of all she loved me. All her messages ended with the same three words that I rewound over and over and over again. *I love you.*

Another obsessive habit I manifested on my wanderings was drawing. I started to draw on napkins, receipts, tables, etc. I'd use condensation as my medium on rain-slick windows. My fingers were a brush against a soft slut's ass.

I never used to have an artistic bone in my body. I only

maintained decent stick figures that would be sufficient for organic chemistry, but not for Pictionary.

Now I have filled sketchbooks. Now I have hours and hours of logged meditative focus.

After the accident, I started to get migraines that only escalated with each day. Meditation helped me refocus away from any mental pain.

I sketched women in different types of thickness and curves. I also sketched a few nature scenes. For every one tree, there were at least five women sketched within the bounds of my sketchbooks. I sketched until the ink ran out.

At first, my sketches of women were anatomical. Hands became arms and bodies. The different images of women steeped in my mind. With time the women became one woman. I drew the same delicate face with small features and blazing turquoise eyes, luscious lips, and flushed cheeks.

A few months passed, and it became blatantly obvious that I could not keep a job. My mind was racked with an obsession over the woman I conjured up in my mind. She was 'the lady of my mind'—the mental hypocorism of endearment being Lady.

The clearer her lines and shades became on paper, the more forgetful and clumsy I became in reality. Start times were like suggestions. Customer service with a smile was downright laughable. Showers were negotiable. Lady was always present in my frontal lobe—like a tumor redirecting my decisions. Blue skies were turquoise eyes.

Casinos were my safe place. Time passed with no windows or easily accessible exits. Bright lights and a symphony of non-stop kept me non-stop. The swirling gaudy carpet patterns helped me ride the manic wave cresting in me.

Nights never ended. Days never began. I never had to sleep. Flashing lights and whistles had my distraction. A buffet of women in varying forms of undress held my eye.

Casino's wanted me to stay. The casino's kept me safe, kept

the environment the same. There was no judgment. Time held the doors open and still. Lights were always on. Someone was smiling and waiting to see me. "Welcome Hudson," they would say, "Welcome back Mr. Thomas." Welcome back. Welcome. I hope you enjoy your stay.

And I did stay. I won over five thousand dollars the first night I played cards. I also played with the waitress. I brought her back to my room and fucked her blindfolded against the bedroom door.

When I went dark, I didn't allow anyone to see me. Not when my eyes blackened, and I felt 100% connected.

After indulging in my first winnings, when morning crested, I woke up to find Emily (the waitress) flipping through pages of my sketchbook. She stood naked next to the dresser. I only saw her silhouette. The curtains were closed—light came from the bathroom. I shifted and sat up in bed. My brain was two sizes too big for my skull.

"So who's the woman?" Her voice was irritating, shrilly and painful to my hungover senses. I looked at her and wondered how long she's been awake. And more importantly, *why was she still here?*

Instead of asking questions, I responded, "I don't know."

She walked over to me and sat down on the bed. One of my sketchbooks was still in her clutches. With a click, she turned on the bedside lamp.

She was too close to me. Her ass buddied up to my leg. A thin rumpled white sheet separated us.

The lamplight was a spotlight to her already painted face. There's no way she woke up like that.

"These drawings are awfully detailed." She said and leaned closer to inspect my sketches. It looked like she was trying to authenticate my lines and determine if I was a fraud.

I moved away from her, "I have a detailed imagination". Naked, I got out of bed from the other side. Emily's body blocked the light. She was back to being just a silhouette—I preferred her in profile. When she acquired a shape, she gained a voice.

"I don't believe you." She replied.

"I don't care."

She pouted, which made me instantly regret sleeping with her.

I left her to take a shower without another word. I was happy to find she vacated when I returned to the bedroom. Though before she left, she scribbled her number in blue pen under one of my sketches.

Emma, her name was Emma. She scrawled her signature, large and in cursive with two little hearts at the end. I stared at the hearts like they were tiny beating monsters.

"WHISKEY," I said and sensed the waitress' flirtation. The warmth of her blush caressed my neck quickly, like a feline's stretch while turning during a nap—reflexive and transitionary. She'll be back. She's settling in.

I felt her emotions like a sweater or blouse that slips on and off. Before the accident, I would have felt the waitress's intentions like a hot breeze—fleeting and not always telling. Heat may be associated with too many emotions; flirtation, jealousy, passion, greed, etc. I had to rely heavily on body cues.

After the accident, intentions presented themselves as layered and dimensional. Emotions were worn and accessorized in movement. In my mind, the waitress felt like a crushed velvet shawl—opulent, voluminous and sculptural. In one word she was luxurious. She wanted to be around me in a deep embrace.

I watched her get orders from the card players around me before disappearing into the crowd. She wrote nothing down.

I rubbed my gritty eyes and waited.

The waitress was by my side handing me a whiskey within a handful of minutes. "Would you like anything else, Mr. Thomas?"

Her name-tag read Annie. I took a sip and said, "No thank you, Annie." I repeated Annie a couple more times in my head to help my memory retain her name. Her name was Annie.

"All right Mr. Thomas, let me know if you do." Her hand trailed along my shoulders when she walked away.

Just as Annie was getting lost in the crowd, she looked over her shoulder and caught me watching. She smiled wide and bright. Her luscious figure tossed her hips from side to side with more emphasis. She was preening from my attention. Each sway was a purr.

My attention turned back to my cards, and I played hand, after hand, after hand, after hand... I lost track of how many hands. My ever-present migraine was heavy with exhaustion. For the past few hours, my brain had a separate throbbing heartbeat.

Then something that's never happened before, happened—I felt a deafening of noise.

Through meditation, I could change the frequency of my migraine to a hum or white noise. I could also soak the noise in alcohol and drugs. My favorite was to fuck it out of my system momentarily. I was never able to mute the noise, not completely. There was always a draining of resources.

Now my attention pulled for the opposite reason—Silence

I passed on a hand I should have raised and looked around myself like the culprit would be a smoking gun and easily detectable. There were masses of people playing and watching. It was a casino; this would be like finding fucking Waldo. I didn't even know what or whom I was searching for. I scanned my surroundings regardless. No one was overtly or suspiciously gawking at me.

I found Annie. She walked through my line of sight and my eyes followed her hips, they lost their heavy sway. She walked towards a table of women. A tray of mixed drinks on her hand. This wasn't her final stop. Most likely her first, there were three women and at least nine drinks on her tray. Two of the women hover over the third. The two I was able to see were beautiful, yet didn't strike my eye. At least not enough to turn my attention away from Annie.

The cluster separated when Annie made it to their table. She passed out a clear drink and a couple of fruity concoctions.

It was when Annie backed away that I saw the third girl who held the clear drink with a lime wedge. Her fingers were thin and slim, the perfect hands for a pianist. Henna decorated her left hand but not her right.

I recognized her immediately.

My body stilled.

I lost my breath.

It was like I was looking at my favorite author or musician. I knew all her vulnerabilities, and she knew nothing about me. This couldn't be real life. Famous people aren't real. She isn't real. The third girl—the hidden girl, was from my sketches—she was Lady. Medium height with skin white as snow. Long blue-black hair hid her face. Her lean body and full lips wore blood red. She was the most beautiful of the three.

My body moved before I registered what I was doing.

It was as though I spent my whole life playing lovers' telephone and she finally picked up the other tin can. The string grew taut, and I responded instantly. I had a direct line to her. I've never been so fully aware or connected to someone in my life.

Walking at a normal pace was a struggle. Bystanders stood in my way like pins. I had to verify the girl wasn't a lookalike to Lady. I had to know that I wasn't going crazy. There was no way this woman was the same as the lady of my mind. *The lady was of my mind.* By definition alone, she couldn't exist.

My neck stretched to look around the human-pins still in my way. Their pink dresses, black high heels, and pink drinks made them look like flamingos.

Lady's face lifted as if she heard my plea. I saw her long eyelashes rise and then her turquoise eyes simmered. A rich and vibrant blue-green like the gem.

It was her.

It was fucking her.

My legs rebelled and streaked straight into the group of flamingo themed human-pins and I spilled their drinks all over them and myself. An accidental strike. Loud shrieks and chaos ensued. Pitches were reached that only babies and small dogs could escalate too. Amongst a smattering of pink, I stood like a pillar.

I reeked of Manhattan's and Sex on the Beach.

With a curse, I left.

Back in my room, I showered off the sticky sweet residue.

My yellow eyes reflected at me in the steam-filled mirror. I dressed in a fresh-pressed hunter green button-up shirt with dark jeans. *Where did I think I was going?*

My hands rushed against my buzzed scalp. It was an odd sensation. A few nights ago, I had a nightmare that wrecked my sheets in sweat. The nightmare was of Terra and the way her fingers used to fiddle and brush through my hair. I panicked, bought a pair of cheap clippers and shed the remains of her fingerprints. The sense memory that loitered in the recesses of my mind was ripped off like a Band-Aid. Or at least I thought.

My reflection looked back at me with my normal pained face.

Then it occurred to me like a sucker punch, Lady muted my brain. For the few minutes I was near her, I felt no pain. For those brief minutes, my body no longer throbbed with two pulses, just one. Nausea had taken a step back, and I could see. I could breathe.

Who the fuck was she? And where the fuck was she now?

I ran through hotels and clubs and only stopped long enough to gauge my pain. My brain still beat with a higher pressure than my heart.

It didn't take long until I fumbled into a club and felt the peacefulness of my mind. As if being baptized and meeting Jesus—or just finishing that first line of cocaine—the tranquility and focus were instant.

She was here. *Thank fuck.*

I sat on a barstool and ordered a whiskey to calm my nerves and catch my breath. As long as my mind was calm, she was near. I didn't have to rush to her.

I wouldn't frighten her.

I'm not a monster.

Terra had me all wrong. *Damnit, how long will it take for my mind to stop resurrecting Terra at every other thought?*

Marty, or Marci was my bartender. Her name-tag was hidden behind her hair. I'd catch a letter or two when she moved. She talked a lot with her hands, but made no drinks.

She stood in front of me and complained of the heat. Everything was hot. It was too hot outside for a smoke break, the air was too hot in here, making drinks made her hot, drinking drinks made her hot, the rug burn she wanted me to give her was hot, etc...

A stool scooted out next to me and someone sat down.

A voice seeped into my bloodstream, "Patron on the rocks with lime please". I felt an instant magnified attraction. A lit match to a gas soaked pile. Instant fire. Even the air was flammable.

Breathe. Deep inhale. And not such a dramatic exhale.

My thoughts tugged and warred with each inflation and deflation of my lungs.

Inhale, *she's sitting next to you*. Exhale, *stop talking to yourself*.

Inhale, *say something*. Exhale, kill her. *Kill her?*

Marty-Marci passed her a glass full of soda water and lime. She then turned back to me ready to list what else made her hot.

"No, I wanted a glass of patron and ice."

Marty-Marci angrily tossed a few limes on a napkin and left. On the way to the Patron, she was distracted by another patron who listened to her heated tales. The Patron was forgotten.

"Figures," Lady murmured to herself.

I leaned forward and signaled for Sandra, a thin redhead who spent time between the sheets with me. She sauntered over to me and licked her lips, "Hey baby, how'd you know I would be working today?"

I didn't, pure coincidence. I leaned closer and laid it on thick. I gave her all the smooth nice words she liked so much. Then I asked her to grab me a bottle of Patron from the back and a glass half-filled with ice. When she returned, I slipped her a hundred-dollar bill and kissed her knuckles like the lady she wasn't, "Thank you".

"Call me, I don't work on Wednesday."

I nodded even though I had no intention of calling. I didn't know what day of the week it was today, let alone how to navigate to Wednesday.

My nod appeased her because she moved down the bar and began taking drink orders. She had to work double since Marty-Marci was on a heated escapade and only hired for her looks.

Without a proper introduction, I opened the bottle and poured Lady's drink.

"Thank you," she said between a smile and turned her full attention towards me. She was far more breathtaking than my sketches. I did her no justice. Her comparison to Snow White was uncanny. The fact that I felt drugged by her only added to the comparison.

"You're welcome." I smiled back at her. I'm sure it looked like a grimace, but I tried to look friendly.

"Has anyone ever asked you if you wear contacts?" I asked trying to make small talk. I sounded as awkward and cliché as I felt. At least I didn't stutter or stab her. I don't understand why knives were on the table as options, but they were. A concerning part of me wanted to stab her. It felt like a survival instinct that she needed to die before me.

"About as often as you're asked I'm sure." She flipped her heavy hair over her shoulder and began to twist it around her hand until it looked like one giant dreadlock. Her hair loosely unraveled but stayed for the most part contained in a spiral. The other side of her neck was bare and exposed.

The part of me that brought knives to the table stared at her neck like it was a spotlit silver platter. I didn't believe in vampires and I didn't believe I was a vampire either, but I could empathize with them at that moment. My body wanted to move into action, but the only verbs it presented were touch, taste, grab, bite. A beast in me needed fed.

I felt the whisper of the need for her turn into a startling scream.

Crash, the stool dropped and rattled behind me.

I was shaking. Thoughts of squeezing the soft skin around her throat circled my mind's drain.

What the fuck was happening to me?

The extremes were like a seesaw. On one side, I wanted passion that was intense and cleansing. I wanted my hands on her. I wanted to squeeze her tight and claim her like a fucking barbarian.

On the other side, I wanted aggression, pain and hurt. A simple shift in weight and murder was in my sights.

I rushed out of the hotel as another surge of snapping vertebras slithered into my thoughts. I vomited on the sidewalk. A pair of white heeled shoes received some over-spray. I apologized, dizzy and clouded.

A spider web of spittle connected me to the pavement. I wiped my face but kept my head between my knees.

I've been violent before. I have gotten in a few fistfights, but they were all posturing. I needed to prove I was right. This sensation that raged within me over Lady was sinister. I didn't want anyone to know. I wanted to kill her with my bare hands. I wanted to end her life in the dark.

My murderous intentions felt right, which in turn made me insane. *Does an insane person know they're insane? Was that even a sane question?*

My migraine resumed residence in my brain when I distanced myself from her. The onslaught was brutal. I went into another fit of vomiting as the escort to the heeled mistress stormed towards me.

"HEY KID!" The large meathead yelled towards my crumpled figure as I heaved every liquid content from my stomach into the bushes. The whiskey burned the insides of my throat. It did not taste better the second time around. Tears pooled in my eyes and impaired my vision.

"I'm going to make you clean her shoes with your tongue."

I couldn't respond. I had just lifted my head when a fist landed square against my upper cheek knocking me sideways. Blood ran down the side of my face. The meathead had multiple rings on each finger, a few now branded my skin and blood. Adrenaline pulsed.

The same fist flew through the air towards me again, and again. The onslaught of pain was well-deserved and helped calm me away from the noise and turbulence of recent events. I wanted to be knocked out of commission so I wouldn't have to suffer. But my pride was unwilling and as I took the fourth punch in stride, I then rose and caught the fifth.

My palm clutched my opponent's hand, my finger's compressed, my grip squeezed, crushing bones. The meathead bellowed for mercy. Rings tinkered to the cement. White heeled shoes crusted with my vomit danced in my vision like the wearer had to urinate. She swung her purse dramatically attacking my torn-up face.

There wasn't a transition between attacks.

"Woman!" I snatched her wrists as gently as I could and she stared at me.

Eye contact.

She screamed a bloody shrill as if I were hurting her. Fear coursed through her and the emotional impact swamped me. There were too many noises, too much pain and emotions in the air. I was overstimulated—my brain was about to bleed and have a full-blown aneurysm.

Before the meathead had an opportunity to rise, I disappeared into a narrow alley.

My hands wiped away the sweat and blood from my face. I tasted the remnants of iron on my tongue and looked down at my shaking hands. My soul was a stone-cold tomb. The brick against my back was hard and comforting. Solid.

I stared at the deep red on my hands as if I've never seen the color before. Dark brown motor oil might as well be coating my skin. It was as though I had momentary colorblindness, red and green were indistinguishable.

Viscous and slowly drying, my blood felt like Lady's blood. My hands didn't feel like my own. *What was happening to me?*

Three drops hit the pavement. They should have been rubies. Instead, the drops looked vile.

I TOOK off my green button-up and wiped myself down. I had a dark shirt on underneath.

Slowly, I stepped back into the public and into the hotel. Thankfully in a town saturated in sinners, no one asked questions. As long as I was upright and bipedal, I was okay.

I kept my eyes on the carpet and stumbled along the walls. I tried to keep to the shadows. The carpet design was too intricate and my eyes crossed. *Was I concussed?* Maybe I moved faster than I realized, like a vehicle that needed an oil change, my steps chugged and stuttered.

Stalled, chugged and stuttered.

Stalled.

A hand clasped around my arm. I stopped and hadn't realized it.

Lady, the same woman I imagined dying by my own hands, gave me forward momentum. Visions of her warm blood dripping like a leaky faucet down and off my fingertips stalked me.

Another wave of nausea.

I wanted to kill her. The thought both repulsed and intrigued me. Up and down, back and forth—my seesaw mentality in action.

Against my will and better judgment, I followed her as any addict would. She pulled me away from the safety of a crowded room and into an isolated elevator. I pressed my floor number and left a bloody fingerprint. Pressing a wadded up shirtsleeve to the button, I tried to rub off the blood and managed to rub off the number entirely and smeared blood on the panel and edges of other buttons. I gave up and pressed back into the corner of the elevator feeling like the embodiment of a murder scene.

We stood staring straight ahead as the numbers counted up. 1,2,3,4...

"Please let go of my arm," I said while we passed floor seven. Her emotions flooded and debilitated me. She had me in a straitjacket, tight, too tight.

The pressure on my arm was removed, and I was left in silence.

The silence I mistook for peace woke up a beast in me I hadn't known was hibernating. The part of me that carried knives and put twisted vertebras on the menu wanted a proper noun. It wanted acknowledgment as a Beast.

And it howled for blood and carnage.

13

SNOW WHITE

HUDSON

THE ELEVATOR DOORS SPREAD. Lady stepped out beside me. The Beast within me rallied in a craze. My fingers tingled for snapped appendages.

I slipped in my keycard, a green light shined and the door opened.

"I've got it from here," I said and started to shut the door. Before the door clasped, Lady slipped in the Patron bottle, "Don't be rude." The glass clinked against the metal striker plate and the door ricocheted back open wide.

"You want to nurse me back to health?" I asked from the entryway.

I wanted more of her. I was a diabetic in a bakery. An alcoholic at the bar. A junkie at their dealer. I wished I had the strength to verbalize my mental status or give words to my confessions of murderous intentions.

I should have lied and stated I was unwell—that I was moments away from puking. My breath would back me up.

Stale vomit formed a film on the inside of my cheeks. My whole being should be an affront to her.

I turned away and walked further into the penthouse. I didn't say another word to her. And I didn't wait for her response.

The choice was hers to make. The decision was in her actions.

I intended to clean myself off. Yet when I heard the click of the door and her soft steps behind me, I knew I couldn't stay away from her. I bypassed the bathroom and went into the kitchen.

This was the first time I stepped foot onto the tiled floors. The only parts of the penthouse I ever used were the master bedroom and bathroom.

Lady walked in behind me and opened almost every cabinet until she found glasses and poured us both a heavy portion of tequila. I rinsed my mouth out at the sink and waited for the accompaniment of doors slamming like dominoes. It never happened, the doors remained open like mouths left ajar. The shelves remained hungry for content while I remained hungry for context.

"I wasn't looking for you in the lobby." She said and slid a glass towards me. The liquid tousled when I clutched and stopped the glass. My hands were tinted with my semi-dried blood, which all too easily transformed into being Lady's blood. And the notion that my hands were the cause of her spilled blood satisfied the Beast. I was possessed.

"Blood makes you squeamish?"

"Yeah, you could say that," I said revealing a strange white lie. It wasn't the blood itself that brought on nausea, but the need to cause her to bleed. I took a few deep breaths, cheers'd the air, tapped the counter, and downed my drink.

I didn't wait for her. I turned back to the sink and began the meditative ritual of washing my hands. The clear water rinsed off the dark bloodstain. Once the water ran clear, I tossed a handful on my face and grunted in pain. The injuries I sustained were worse than I anticipated. Swelling was setting in like insulating foam sealant. My skin was hot to the touch. An additional heartbeat pulsed pain through my injured cheek, nose, jaw, and eye socket.

The pain curbed my murderous intentions.

Why did I have murderous intentions? Why her?

It's like she slammed the door shut on my migraines, but left a doggy door open for the Beast to get in.

"I lost track of my friends, that's how I ran into you." She said while she rummaged through drawers. "You were about to be mobbed by random people and I figured you would prefer to not be... mobbed that is." A drawer slammed shut.

"Do you have a room here?" I asked. Another drawer opened and slammed shut.

The drawers never stayed shut once they slammed, they would pop back open a sliver. Issues never resolved. Conclusions never met.

"Am I really that repulsive to you?" Open, *slam,* and sliver. Open, *slam,* and crack. Open, *slam,* and a touch slipped back open so that the drawer could breathe. "That you can't wait to get rid of me?"

I stood by the sink with my face dripping wet and watched her. I felt her every breath. I felt the air move when she moved. I felt the air being pushed out of each drawer. I felt the air, and I didn't understand. *How could I feel air to this degree?* My senses were rewiring to accommodate the Beast.

I lived my life in only primary colors. Life was yellow, blue or red. Then I met her and she opened a door to a part in me I didn't know existed. She brought green, purple and orange into my life—and they couldn't be taken away. The colors engrained in my DNA.

And the longer I stayed with her, shades and variants like teal, magenta, lavender, and coral revealed themselves.

I wondered if she felt the same way.

How would I explain color to someone who has never seen them? How could I explain the different variations of azure blue, ocean blue, midnight blue, royal blue, sky blue, or dark turquoise that I saw in her eyes?

I wondered also if she had a newly awakened Beast. Because the Beast in me stretched a set of muscles and nerves that fired for the first time. Being near her prompted a muscle memory that was rapidly becoming more attuned to her. I wanted to get in and under her skin in a violent manner.

The dichotomy between my urges to experience more life and to exterminate hers battled within my head. But it warred silently like two individuals in the middle of a heated argument spoken in sign language. The gestures were murderous—the intent combative. The words were silent. I was silent. Face and hands still dripped wet with water. She stood next to me, but I couldn't look at her. My gaze remained on the wide-open cabinets and slightly opened drawers. Lady was a force of nature; she was my cocaine; she was Snow White; she was my Snow.

The faucet turned on and off.

My eyes and thoughts had become my enemies. And as I tried to shut off both circuits a damp dishtowel dabbed my face. I sank to the floor and tried to immobilize myself from ripping her apart. The muscles and nerves she awakened were programmed to shred at supernatural speed with supernatural strength.

"You don't have to be such a baby. I barely touched you." She said as she squatted down to my level.

"I'm not a baby. You're oblivious to what I'm going through."

During all my sketches, I only felt an obsession to find her. In the flesh, with her in all her three-dimensional glory... Now I only ached for her destruction.

Slowly she patted my swollen, bloody face clean. "There, now you're somewhat presentable."

"Thank you. I could have done that myself."

"Aren't you sincere?" She got to her feet and headed down a path towards the master bedroom—where I left my sketchbooks. Where my sketchbooks were naked, bared-open, on my bed.

I'm on my feet and in front of her, "Where are you going?"

"I'm looking for a first aid kit."

"I'm fine."

"You're split open. I can literally see inside you."

My hands pressed firmly against the doorframes. There was strictly no admittance.

She tossed her hands up in defeat and backed away with a smirk. My eyes followed her hips. The thin red fabric of her dress left nothing to the imagination. She was about to round the corner into the kitchen when I whispered in exasperation under my breath, "Fuck me."

My words were for my ears only, but she heard me. She shouldn't have been able to hear me. From the kitchen she asked, "What did I do this time to irritate you?"

"Moved. How'd you know I was watching?" Maybe she didn't hear me.

"Because I was walking."

She came back into the hallway with her drink and took a sip of Patron, "I'm not allowed to touch you, and now I'm not allowed to move."

"Not too hard to follow."

"Why are there so many restrictions? Are you scared of me?"

"Terrified."

She moved closer, and I backed away maintaining the same distance between us.

"What are you going to do about it?"

"Nothing..." I was in limbo between cutting off her life and taking her up in my arms. *How could I possibly articulate that?*

She walked outside to the patio. Las Vegas was alive with light. No stars had a chance to shine.

I walked out behind her. She stood at the railing and stared down at the pulse of the sinful city.

"What's your name?" I asked from the shadows.

She looked around for me, but couldn't see me. I gained comfort from being able to see her while she couldn't see me. Stalking her helped curb my freshly found impulses.

I have truly turned into a sick fuck.

"Aviana." Her voice sank into me like molasses, heavy, deep, completely saturating and rich.

"What's your name?" She asked me with her arms folded around the stone railing. She looked at the strip below, outwardly ignoring me. But I felt her interest. Her piquing curiosity was like a poker used to tend a fire.

"Hudson."

"Are you always this unusual Hudson?"

"Just with you."

"Why is that?"

"What I feel for you isn't natural." Because I'm desperate to break every bone in your body, didn't slip out between my lips.

"It feels natural." Her voice, velvet soft as the night itself caressed my newly awakened nerves.

"Don't say that."

She turned with aggravation blazing in her eyes, "Why?"

I stepped out of the deep shadows against my better judgment. The darkness split me in half.

Her eyes found me—she looked at me like she could see all my colors. I took another step closer to her. Fully engulfed by the moonlight.

"Where are you from?" She asked while she took a tantalizing step towards me.

"Nowhere I'm willing to go back to. Where do you live?" I didn't move, but I tensed significantly.

"Washington."

"Where are you staying tonight?" My voice went back to my cold, business demeanor.

"Paris."

"I'll walk you to your hotel."

The walk wasn't too long, but it felt like an eternity since neither of us spoke.

Once in the lobby of the Paris hotel, she pressed the button to call the elevator.

The elevator descended; it was three floors away.

Two floors away.

One floor away.

Then the elevator doors slid open.

She stepped inside, turned, and stared directly back—her eyes asked me, *Do I want to see you again?*

MY RESOLVE only lasted four hours.

The receptionist, Barb, reprimanded me like a mother of at least five. "Sir, I don't know how many times I have to tell you that I **cannot** reveal guest information. Leave a note." A pen and stationery pad were slapped towards me like a hockey puck in an air hockey game.

Barb didn't understand that *my air* was upstairs—she simply continued *click-clacking* on her keyboard. My hand clamped down on the pad and kept it from falling off the low friction lobby counter.

"I can't write what I want to say."

Barb moved her mouse, "Don't you reckon if she was interested she would have told you where she was staying?" She made a few clicks, then made eye contact. "If you would like, I may reserve you a room, or you can write a note."

"Barb, *will you marry me,* isn't anything I can leave on a note."

Barb stopped typing. "I suggest; will you call me, first."

I scribbled, please call me and indicated my room number and cell phone number. I folded the missive in half and passed the puck back.

"I will gladly pass the message to Aviana... what is her last name?"

"I don't know. But there can't possibly be that many Aviana's in your system."

"I'm not a magician." She said and placed the note by her keyboard and continued to type like I didn't exist.

I went back to my room and burned holes in the carpet pacing. The night transitioned into day and then night again. My eyes were a constant black. I moved from chair to chair in every room. I sat on every cushion. I lied on every mattress. I paced to every object, touched and threw every movable piece.

Why didn't she come back? Did she know?

I smashed everything besides the Patron bottle. *What would I do if she did show up now? In this disaster zone?*

Anger filled me. *What did I expect?* I kicked her out of my room and now I'm begging her to come back so I could do what? Not look at her. Not touch her. I screamed in bizarre agony and punched the mirror. My expression was demonic in the shattered glass.

In my bedroom, I heard my cell phone ringing. Instantly I was there.

"Hello?"

I fell onto the comforter of my bed and closed my eyes for the first time— and saw Aviana with blood streaking down her face. My eyes tore open even though they burned to remain closed.

"Hey," a male voice from my past said. It was Ben. It wasn't her.

129

"I've been trying to reach you for weeks man. I tried your folks, and then in desperation, I even asked Terra. Finally, I talked to Mickey, and he gave me your new number, listen, man, I need a favor." Ben said in the middle of a crowd. I could barely understand what he was saying.

"What?"

"I'm short on cash and I signed a contract to an apartment. I need you to come help me out and live with me for a few months."

"As long as you're not on the west coast I'll be there." I felt hard of hearing. I wasn't sure what I was agreeing to, but the fear and loathing in Las Vegas scene was played out.

"Delaware."

"Delaware?"

"Come on man, give it some respect, it's the first state."

"Text me the address."

I STEPPED out of a cab and onto the curb of an antique three-story red house. My head tipped back, and I took in the monstrosity my friend purchased. The house nestled just outside campus.

The cab honked its departure. Ben stampeded out of the house agile and every bit as tall and lean as the last time we saw each other. He lacked a shirt and barely had his sweatpants tied.

I slung my bag over my shoulder. "I thought you said you rented an apartment?"

I played a few high stakes games before leaving Vegas and managed to pay for the damages and have a considerable sum left over.

"My bad man." Ben laughed a husky laugh. We walked up the brick steps and through the front door, "I spent too much money renovating and am coming up short on bills. Should we talk finances or should I just ask for a check?"

I dropped my bag on the fresh wood floor of the foyer and passed a stack of crisp twenties to Ben.

The house's inside was every bit as large as it seemed from the curb with narrow hallways that slithered into secret passageways. A vintage house from the 1900s that riddled with rooms. Intricacies and crown molding were everywhere.

"This house is insane."

"Shhhh...... Don't call her names, you'll stub your toe or come up missing," Ben said as he slapped two hands on my shoulders. "Your room is upstairs at the end of the hallway, mines the first on the right. The rest of the house is fair game and under construction." Ben ran up the stairs before I could ask any more questions. A minute later, I heard female voices.

I took the steps two at a time—and as I rounded the corner to the hallway I heard muffled pleas for a Ninja. The only Ninja Ben had going for him was the stereotypical kind with his ethnicity. Or the blender, I hoped he had the Ninja blender.

At the end of the hall, I found the door open to a stark white room. I dropped my bag. The fan sifted through the air. The room still smelled of fresh paint. There was a king sized bed with white sheets and a white down comforter with four white pillows. I took a deep breath and plunked myself down on the blankets in hopes of sleep.

My eyes burned to remain closed, but I couldn't stop the violent images from pulsating across the front lines of my mind. After tossing and turning I took out my sketchbook, opened it to a blank page, and started to draw. I drew Aviana's smile and her mischievous eyes when she overheard me at my penthouse. When I finished, I tore the sheet off and taped it to the wall at eye level. She held secrets, and I wanted to know them. I wanted to know all of her.

Again, I tried to close my eyes and when I opened them in

fear, I saw her smiling at me. Everything was going to be okay. She's smiled back at me, alive and bright and on the west coast. I'll find her secrets once I figured mine out.

I repeated this process several times until I finally fell into a fitful sleep, which was more of an unconsciousness.

Downstairs Ben paraded around the kitchen.

"Ninja," I said in sarcastic greeting and sat down at the barstool. Ben laughed with a large sub in his hands that he used as a mock samurai sword.

"Hudson," Ben said with the sub at my neck, "Terra was wondering how you were doing,".

I pushed the sub aside, "I'm sure she just asked to be polite."

"I don't think it was out of a courtesy man."

"I don't want to talk about Terra."

"Well, Terra had an awful lot of questions about you."

"I don't care."

"She does." Ben took a large bite of his sub and pulled the stool out next to me prepared to hash out my past with my ex-everything.

I didn't want to have this conversation with Ben, or with anyone. Not even with myself.

Ben kicked his feet up on the stool's footrest while I kicked mine off.

"Great, that's great. I'm going to take myself for a walk."

I left Ben alone in the kitchen and left with a chip on my shoulder.

I found myself at the local university library. It was old with thick brick walls that cut off the signal to my cell phone. Concentrated murmurs and turning pages filled the dim corridors. Even though there was still constant noise in my head, the noise was focused and less disturbing. When I looked at students, I saw masses of hunkered down parkas—they were waiting for the storm to pass with hot beverages and Cold War stories. They would rather be anywhere else, but they've procrastinated too long.

I sank myself into a dark leather couch and people watched. It became a game for me to wander until I found minuscule comfort. Libraries, dog parks, and centers where groups prayed in unison were common winners. University libraries were my favorite, with their 24/7 access to knowledge, snacks, and caffeine.

An hour later, I woke up with an overwhelming sensation of peace. Which matched a pairing dose of fear, if I was at peace... The reality of the situation sank in.

14

COMMON GROUNDS

HUDSON

The Beast in me roared to the forefront. *What fucking happened to Washington?*

My zip-up hoodie hung off-kilter on my shoulders. The worn carpet softened the heavy blows of my feet. I prowled the aisles. The crusty sleep in my eyes forgotten. I checked all the study holes. Aviana wasn't on any floor above ground. But she was here. And as I took the steps to the basement, my heart raced.

I paused on my third step down. The humane part of me slowed my transgressions. As much as I wanted to face her, I couldn't with the murderous thoughts that surged through me. Nothing changed. She brought the Beast out in me. I refuse to be recognized as a monster. Any fear from her would be a tsunami compared to the ripple of emotions I'm accustomed from others. She could wash me out entirely.

I retracted my steps and went back to the house. My migraine came back like a hammer slammed into a sheet of paper, no resistance, I blacked out in the kitchen with the fridge door wide open.

Whoosh. Splash. "Fuck!" I yelled. I woke to Ben pouring freezing water on my face. Water was in my nose and lodged in my throat. Drowning on dry land, I coughed and sputtered.

"I'm sorry man," Ben said and placed the empty pitcher on the floor beside me. He stayed crouched down near me, not quite standing, yet not quite kneeling either. "You weren't waking up, and you were freaking me out."

"I must have passed out."

"Drinking already?"

I wiped my face off with my shirt. "No, I don't know what's been going on with me." My aggressiveness ripped a scab off my cheekbone like wax removes hair with a strip. "FUCK!" I sat up and leaned against the now closed fridge door. I grabbed my shirt from between my shoulder blades and removed it. My face fell into my shirt wrapped hands.

"Man..." Ben drawled out. His knees cracked as he stood to his full height. "I wasn't expecting for you to look like a fucking battered woman."

The faucet turned on and water flowed into a metal pot. I heard the click of the stove turning on. *Smack.* The pot skids on the stove.

"I wasn't even going to say anything, but, man, I can't be worrying about you passing out. What the fuck is going on?" A plethora of sticks were dropped into the water-filled pot.

"Move over," Ben said and I rise to a height slightly taller than his stature. My blood seeped through my shirt and ingrained the cotton fibers into my cut.

Ben opened the fridge and pulled out different ingredients for a pasta dinner.

"Your darkness is out of control. Go take a shower, put a fucking smile on your face and I'll fix us some dinner."

I did what Ben said and returned to the kitchen twenty minutes later.

"Start talking."

I slumped into a chair at the kitchen table and started a story made of white lies. I didn't lie about the fight, but I did downplay the fact that I crushed the bones of my assailant's hand. Aviana had no name in my story, and my sketches never existed. Instead, I focused on my "anger" issues and how some days I was like the incredible hulk in the body of a nomad.

Ben was halfway through eating his spaghetti—a forkful of noodles suspended chin level. "What do the doctors say?" He asked and ate the pending mouthful.

"I don't know doctor, what do you say?"

Ben smiled, and we spent the rest of the dinner going over a list of projects.

Ben's spaghetti hit the mark. We broke garlic bread and talked of the good ole' days. It was nice as long as I didn't look at him. It was a family reunion minus my favorite family member. Terra was absent, and with all the empty chairs around us, it couldn't have been more obvious.

For the next two months, I helped Ben with his house projects. I still drew, just not as much. Not as obsessively. I became less obsessed and more controlled. I meditated.

The nomad became a hermit. My health improved, and I gained more color and muscle. I felt a deeper level of relaxation and could sift through the daily noise in my head.

The Beast and I introduced ourselves to each other, we broke our own bread and compared notes. It wasn't quite the meeting of the minds. The Beast wasn't leashed. But at least it wasn't free reigning either.

THE UNIVERSITY's library was a beacon to my wayward soul.

Yet I haven't visited its borders for the past two months. I told myself it was the books that called to me. The tranquility of thick walls and focused minds. The spotlit sanctuary's call had nothing to do with Aviana.

And as the days fell off the calendar, the call grew louder and louder until I found myself in a sludge deep enough that I couldn't distinguish my ass from my face. No amount of meditation pulled me out of my stupor. Ben kept checking in on me from a distance like my mood was contagious. He started inviting his friend Ramona to check in on me too. His worry grew exponentially, as did the visits from Ramona. If I wasn't going to talk to him, then I had to talk to someone. All Ramona wanted to talk about were my feelings. How did it feel to be so tired? Was my candle lit from both ends? How did it feel to have my candle lit from both ends? Did this feeling remind me of other feelings? And how did that make me feel? How did I truly feel, deep down in my gut? Sometimes she'd pat my stomach like I wouldn't be able to find it without her.

Everyone I knew in Delaware was talking about me, to me, through me. Ben and Ramona circled me like vultures. I stared at them both like they were common starlings and I continued about my tasks.

Ben was far too much; he was an entire football team in one being. The coach, captain, and defensive line stared at me from behind his brown eyes. A parade of cheerleaders cycled in and out of the house. Since the team of Ben was preoccupied with me, the chipper cheerleaders touched my arm and consoled me as superficially as they could tweet.

Ramona with her canary yellow hair was an eccentric mumu out of the 60s. She wanted to surround me, touch my vibes and tell me everything would be groovy again. She wasn't suffocating like Aviana, she was a size too large and all-encompassing. Sometimes I'd get lost in all her fabric and folds. For the most part, there was too much space for me to feel her out.

There was too little space for her to feel me. And there was just enough space for me not to want to tell her about my true feelings.

Eventually, the house was finished and immaculate. All the walls were varying shade of grays and blues. The six bedrooms remained white and the wood floors were dark. Random colorful accents spotted around the house. A golden T-Rex erupted from a guest bathroom. A red ceramic stag hung above the fireplace mantel. A dark green Ping pong table was in the dining room.

I stood in the foyer before the front door with my hands in my pockets. Ben came up behind me. He tossed his arm around my shoulders and said, "Hey man, it's a pretty riveting white door we've got right there."

I nodded. My palms were sweating out all my sins.

"You thinking about going through it? It's been a while since you've taken yourself for a walk." Now we both stared at the door. It was a sharp-looking door.

"I think I'm going to watch Snow," I said. My jaw ticked with the impulse. The longer I'm away from Aviana, the less I saw her as my Lady, and the more she became Snow White, or the most addictive version, Snow.

"I don't think it's snowing yet."

The door opened and Ramona stomped through. Cold rain dripped off her nose. Her cheeks were rosy and wet.

"Fuck it's cold outside," Ramona said as she shook out of her jacket. I grabbed the door before it closed and walked outside into the rain smattered streets.

"Where's he going?"

Ben shrugged. "He wants to watch it snow."

"Does he know it's not snowing?"

At the end of the brick walkway, I turned with rain-slicked hair. Ramona and Ben stood beside each other like two doting parents. In their eyes, I wasn't making smart choices.

"Don't wait up," I yelled and waved my goodbye. I couldn't take another mental shakedown. I didn't understand how I felt, but I knew I wanted to finally check out the basement. Or the Beast did. I wasn't sure who was leading who, but we were going.

I met the library's polished door handles and swung them open.

Quickly I realized there was no Aviana. I went straight to the basement anyway. There was hardly anyone here. I pulled my phone out of my pocket, it read 9:26 pm Friday, November 18. Of course, no one was here, they had better things to do. I, on the other hand, did not.

I took a seat in a corner sofa chair and grabbed a discarded book. I flipped the book around to read its cover; a book of poems by Robert Frost. I read until my brain was heavy with subliminal messages. The words slurred and slushed into one long, long, phrase.

I dozed off. My head tipped down and my body relaxed by section. My eyes grew droopy. My fingers relaxed, and the book slipped.

Gravity pulled.

My reflexes were quick. The Beast shifted my gears, my fingers clutched the pages before the book hit the dirty carpet. I sat up straight and looked around to see if anyone noticed.

One girl did. Blood blossomed on her cheeks. Her eyes widened. I wasn't supposed to catch her watching me.

But now that I had, her eyes glittered.

In my mind's eye, she wore a bright red knit sleeveless shirt that collared into a turtleneck. She wanted to be seen, but she didn't understand what she was doing. Her arms were free and freezing.

She smiled at me in a way that said she wanted to give me a blowjob and then go post on social media about it.

No one else was around.

Hundreds of books witnessed. And though books weren't human, they probably held more personality than the girl who sat a few tables away. Definitely more identity.

She stared at me long passed a socially acceptable interval. I felt I had to acknowledge her existence, so I nodded and walked away with my book of poems—it was awkward and obligatory.

I walked down a few aisles until I reached a table at the back of the basement.

I sat down and tossed my elbows up on the surface and went back to reading words that formed in a straight line and held meaning. Frost took me down his roads before inevitably I dozed off again.

In my dream, I felt an instant weight off my shoulders—like I had been suffering from congested sinus pressure and someone snipped my head off.

My hands reached for my head, but it wasn't there. My hands connected in an awkward high-five.

I lost my head.

And like a helium-filled balloon on its way to a pile of fluffy white clouds, my separated head floated upwards. My eyes watched from above, from the perspective of the clouds.

My segmentation had no effect on my sensations. I saw life through my eyes and touched through my body.

I was still in the library, but the ceiling didn't exist. It looked like a tornado leveled off the floors. The cavernous basement was full of people.

Medusa-like tentacles sprouted out of my neck and touched each individual's head. The end of my tentacles were four-inch needles which pierced through heads like a pin through a corkboard.

I was into everyone's business, into everyone's thoughts. I heard confessions and secrets that I had no business knowing. A man bought used heels to masturbate to. He also regularly donated his sperm to fertility clinics. He'd caress the specimen cup and call his sperm his babies. "Hush" he'd tell the technician, "the babies are sleeping."

A girl hit a bicyclist and drove off. She blamed the damage to her vehicle on a drunk driver.

Another girl habitually steals their coworkers' lunches and then feeds off the water cooler gossip about the asshole thief.

A man failed PE in grade school.

Another man in the corner carried scissors in his back pocket to make raping women easier.

I jumped awake.

The wooden chair I sat in fell on its back with a loud crash. I was on my feet and searching for the corner in my dreams—for the rapist. The library was still mostly empty, and the ceiling held firm above me. White and cracked.

My hands went to my head—as if it were questionable if it were still attached—it was. A few random people were looking at me. I was a disturbance. I couldn't agree more.

I sat back down. They went back to their notes.

The man wasn't there. *Fuck that was too realistic.*

The lost girl from before sat on the far side of the table in front of me. She asked if I was okay. I didn't respond because Aviana sat at the same table.

"Nightmare?" Aviana asked with a smirk. A set of noise-reducing headphones wrapped around her neck. I walked over to her table and sat across from her. She looked the exact same and yet entirely different.

"I wouldn't use that word." I said before I asked, "I wasn't snoring, was I?"

She laughed a laugh that melted my veins.

"You were snoring." Confirmed the lost girl. Awesome. The stairs felt miles away.

My fingers rapped against the table. I've never felt so intensely bipolar in my decision-making.

Only with her.

"Struggling, today?" Aviana asked.

"Every day," I said and soaked in the peace that only she could bring. The Beast did laps around my brain. Salivating, not yet snarling. The Beast and I had an agreement to play with our prey.

"Hey, don't I know you?" The lost girl asked Aviana. I completely forgot lost girl existed. Lost girl looked surprised, her whole body shifted towards Aviana. They sat on the same side of the table, just on opposite ends.

Aviana looked at lost girl, then looked at me. Before she could respond, lost girl added, "You look familiar."

"I do porn." Aviana deadpanned. My eyes widened.

"No, you don't."

"I don't?" Aviana shrugged her shoulders and left without another word.

"She doesn't," lost girl said with a beet red complexion. Lost girl's feet tapped on the worn carpet. Her body was now directed towards me.

"How would you know?" I asked but didn't stay to instigate, after Aviana cleared the corner, I got up and gave chase. Outside of the library and on the public sidewalk I blended with the crowd. Pounding the pavement, the Beast and I were in sync. For the first time, we worked on the same team. The thrill of the hunt fed us both. Whether Aviana would look over her shoulder—it was addictive.

Aviana's headphones brandished her ears like ears muffs. Her head bobbed up and down every few beats. Her lips never formed the words to sing along.

I wanted to know what she listened to. I wanted to know if it was a song I've heard before. Music is the connection between sounds and the soul. If I knew what she listened too, I would have one way to connect with her.

I would have a piece of her soul.

The concept of having a piece of her soul had me thrumming my fingers together like an evil genius. I wanted a piece of her soul. I wanted her.

Aviana dipped out from the crowd and walked into the woods behind McHenry Hall. In the middle of a patch of oak trees, she stopped and sat on a fallen oak comrade.

Her head bobbed more when she was alone. She felt more into herself alone in the trees. The straightjacket I felt her as, infinitesimally loosened a notch. The buckle released and granted breath for a moment.

When I looked at Aviana, I saw the most complex woman I've ever met. I doubted she even knew herself. All I saw was a straightjacket held together by dozens of buckles. Reading her was like getting to the smallest Matryoshka doll, and each doll was a version of herself she created, buried and then buckled in a straightjacket and hexed with riddles.

If I didn't know what had a head, a tail, and was brown, and had no legs, I couldn't unbuckle a notch on the straightjacket.

If I didn't know what had six faces (but wore no makeup) and twenty-one eyes (but can't see), I wouldn't get to the next Matryoshka doll.

The answer to the first was a penny. The second answer was a die. Those were only two answers and the nesting dolls were at least twenty deep.

A few minutes passed while I watched Aviana rummage around her bookbag. Finally, she smiled and pulled out a joint. I didn't see her pull a lighter out. She curled around the joint like a human windshield. A moment later smoke billowed out like a signal for me to move closer.

Carefree and relaxed, she laid down against the trunk.

I watched her in silence and wrestled with the Beast and our need to attack her. Each puff of smoke sent a quiver down my spine. I was a racehorse at the starting gate biding time.

I took slow deep breaths behind a tree in an attempt to dissipate the violent and confused energy within me by concentrating on the smooth ripples of smoke.

I watched her full lips slip around the joint paper. I thought about physics and meditative pathways. I couldn't destroy the Beast. It was a part of me. I didn't understand my murderous nature, but I didn't need to in order to acknowledge its existence and tendencies. I only needed to accept it.

Energy can't be destroyed, only redirected.

The longer I studied the contours of Aviana's lips, the easier a plan for redirection took root.

THE NEXT COUPLE of weeks blurred. I picked up a routine of actively stalking Aviana. I had no shame but kept it to myself.

I toyed with my range of control over the Beast, some days were more violent than others.

I watched her study for hours upon hours of chemistry, physics, and biochemistry. Other days I found her with nature, ecology and local history texts. She never attended any classes. I don't think she was even enrolled as a student. Her apartment was within walking distance to the library and her job. She worked at a trendy bookstore. Ninety percent of the customers that left the bookstore while she was on the clock left with cheesed out grins and no books—they purchased weed and not words.

Public places were the easiest locations to be in with Aviana. All the passionate and violent acts I wanted to perform, I needed to do them in private. If we stayed in public, the option for harm was off the table. Usually, the Beast and I followed that golden rule.

Today was different. Stalking lost its edge. I wanted to claw myself inside her. I sat four tables behind Aviana on the library's second floor. The room was filled with students and tables. Each long table had multiple table lamps installed. Most were turned on even though there was daylight flooding through the windows. I was the only one that sat with nothing in front of me and no baggage beside me.

Fifteen minutes later I stood beside Aviana with two cups of hot coffee and cleared my throat. She nearly jumped out of her seat. Her organic chemistry model set hit the floor.

I collected tiny gray bonds and atoms from the ground while she dropped verbal bombs, "What are you doing here?"

"I brought you coffee," I said. I wasn't about to divulge my extracurricular stalking habits, just the announcement of coffee.

I pulled out sugar and cream packets from my pocket. "It's black."

She took a couple of sugars and added it to one of the cups. She thanked me suspiciously. The coffee wasn't drugged—I thought about it. Cyanide does resemble a nutty sugar to the palette. I could have said it was hazelnut coffee. Antifreeze is sweet. I could have told her I had already added sugar to her coffee.

Aviana took a nervous drink and went back to her studying —blatantly ignoring me.

I sat down across from her and pulled out a small portable sketchbook that I kept in my back pocket. We sat in silence for a couple of hours while she studied and I sketched.

"What are you drawing?" She asked.

I placed my pen between the pages like a bookmark. "An obsession of mine. It helps clear my head if I can visualize it and get it on paper."

"May I see it?"

"It's personal, like a journal. Would you let me read your diary?"

"No, but I don't have one."

"Would you tell me all your secrets?"

She paused and thought about her response like I gave her

hard spearmint to roll around in her mouth, both fresh and spicy.

"Not intentionally." She said and went back to her notes and books.

The next few days we followed the same routine. I stepped out of the shadows and spent longer periods of time with her.

We walked through the woods and smoked joints until they smoldered against our fingertips. Our time was spent in the library. Some of it was spent at her work. All of our time was in public.

Our friendship was classic like denim—casual and dependable. I was uncomfortable without her and would search and search until I found her. In a sea of jeans, I only wanted her. Each day I tried on our friendship one leg at a time. Most days it was a perfect fit. Others were just out of the dryer, hot and too tight. I couldn't bend or move without feeling the Beast about to bust out.

LAST REQUEST

15

REMINISCING

"HEY, Av, Terra and I are about to head out to the grocery store. You coming?" Ben asks from the entryway of Hudson's room. *Or is it considered my room now?* My only addition to the simple guest room is my bookbag that sits by the dresser. Yoga pants are half thrown up from the zipper's mouth. Otherwise, the room remains the same.

Terra honks the horn from inside the Honda that idles in the driveway waiting for its passenger. Carbon monoxide billows from its ass-end. The compound isn't naturally occurring. Neither I believe is Terra.

I'm cocooned in bed with blankets curled up tight beneath my chin. The digital clock on the nightstand is flipped upside down. It reads wa 11:80.

"Did Hudson ever tell you why he flips clocks over?" I ask and push my hair out of my face and back into the bird's nest on top of my head.

With a heavy sigh, Ben leaves his post at the doorway and comes to sit on the edge of the bed. He flips the clock right-side up. "Hudson said time is a human concept, and he didn't want any part of it."

I flip the clock back upside down, "He told me he wanted to live without minutes and live in the moment."

Ben nods his head with a tender expression. His eyes shine like a child who is knuckles deep in slime. The gelatinous memory pulls. "Why do you really think he flipped the clock?"

"I think he did it because he's an addict." I roll over to my back and continue, "He never talked about anything long-term. Conversations about the future overwhelmed him. Everything had to be taken day by day, and sometimes minute by minute."

Ben folds over resting his elbows on his knees, "He always seemed to be battling his demons. That's why I invited Terra for the Halloween party. She was his worst demon. I wanted them to talk it out. Get back to how they used to be." *Get back to being together*. He doesn't say it aloud, but he confirms my worst fears.

Ben continues nostalgically talking to the carpet fibers about *remember when* and *this one time* that actually happened multiple times.

I can't blame him for the desire to get the gang back together. Ben's an only child—raised by his strong single mother. He's the son that every other mother adopted. He's Hudson's brother. Terra's his sister. There's a familial loyalty that isn't defined by blood origins.

Pau and Hudson are the only ones who have ever claimed me. Even then, it was from a distance. And even then, it did me no favors, Pau is dead thanks to me, and Hudson.... *Fucking Hudson*.

The fan above me oscillates and Ben's stories begin to drone into the whirl. Terra honks again from the Honda in the driveway.

Ben pats my leg like he's finishing a thought or placing a bookmark in his memories and says, "Well, I should take off before Terra leaves without me."

I nod, "See you."

He leaves and I hear him parade down the stairs. The car

door slams louder than the front door did. The Honda rolls out and they're gone.

I turn and look at the sketch of my face. "What's the best-case scenario?" I ask my likeness.

"Hudson comes back." I turn onto my back again. If Hudson comes back, he'll be prosecuted for what he did to Genevieve. He'll have to explain the Beast.

FRETFUL.

Ben left the room, yet his words—their spirit linger. The ghosts of Ben's memories invite mine for musings. I'm unsettled and restlessly kick my legs—this isn't a reverie.

The cabin was like the one that burned down. I planned a retreat and wanted the weekend to be a romantic getaway. Hudson, on the other hand, was concerned—and his worry kept him at a distance. It was the same song and dance. The lyrics and scenery were different, but the beats were the same. The bass and pulse of our words were filled with unrequited longing.

"Please sit with me." I appealed from the kitchen table. Hudson sat in the living room on the floor with his plate. It was the second night. The first night he slept on the couch in the living room while I slept in the bedroom. Hudson started in bed with me, but once I fell asleep, he snuck off to the couch.

Fed up with food and Hudson's dissonance I got up and threw my food away. My coleslaw made a sticky, vomit noise when it hit and dripped down the plastic trash bag liner.

"If I knew you were going to act like this, I wouldn't have bothered," I complained as I washed my paisley designed plate. This cabin and myself were trapped in the sixties.

"I told you, I don't know how many times," Hudson said from the living room. I heard him move into the kitchen behind me. He stood with the counter between us, "It's not safe for us to be alone together. If you scream in your apartment, there's Genevieve. And the walls are thin. Paramedics can reach you quickly. Here, there's no one for miles. You could bleed out before any help arrives. I could have you buried. How many people even know you're here?"

"Why the fuck would I be bleeding?" I asked calmly and manhandled my hair behind my ears and scrubbed my clean plate. Bubbles clung to the strands of my hair and stuck to my forehead and earlobe.

"Because I'm dangerous. I can hurt you." He said like he was explaining how $1+1=2$. Common sense, *what was wrong with me?* I heard $0.2 + -8 + 4.6 + 0.5 + 3.7 + 1 = 2$. It wasn't as simple as he portrayed it to be.

"I don't think you'll hurt me," I said exhausted by the mental math of our non-linear conversation.

"You don't know what it feels like. I want to hurt you. I almost need to hurt you. The Beast..."

"I trust you not to. And you haven't. We're arguing over hypotheticals."

"You're crazy. You can't trust me. I don't even trust me."

"I'm crazy... We're name calling now?" I take my clean plate out of the sink and smash it on the floor like we're at a Greek wedding. Sniffling and doing a really shitty job of holding back tears, "I'm fucking crazy."

The faucet ran heavy with hot water. I watched the water go straight down the drain.

Hudson came up behind me and wrapped his arms around my waist without making a sound. He nuzzled my neck and said, "Let's go back to your apartment."

I turned the water off. I shut myself off too. Drained and tired of the steps we take in our dance. I backed away and said, "Right, you're probably right. I'll go get my things together from the room."

Hudson busied himself cleaning his plate. I left the broken

ceramic shards where they laid. A fake watery smile plastered on my face. When I walked away, it felt like the start of our end.

I walked into the bathroom and gathered my toiletries. With my toothbrush in hand, I watched a solitary tear track down my face in the mirror. I looked heartbroken. I was heartbroken.

I wiped my face and went back to the kitchen.

Again, the faucet was on full blast. Steam rose from the basin as the water pounded the stainless steel. Hudson stood in front of the rushing water, just as I had—equally drained, if not more so. Plate in his left hand, sponge in his right. The plate couldn't get any cleaner. Hudson rubbed against the paisley design like it personally insulted him.

Except inanimate objects don't insult, people do.

I did. I do it all the time.

We swapped our pasts, but he expected more out of me. For instance, picking up the broken shards, *why didn't I do that?*

Our connection was intense. Too intense, like a live wire or lightening. I wanted to watch the show, *fuck the plate, fuck everything.* I wanted our energy directly. Skin to skin was how we conducted best. Our physiology never lied. And that's all I wanted this weekend. Some skin to skin contact with Hudson.

I pulled my purse higher on my shoulder. Tension had my shoulders raised to my ears. He didn't want me the same way.

"Huds-," I started.

"It's just a bad day today *Snow*. We'll get through it." He said at my carotid artery. My back against the wall. His hot, bubble laden hands pushed me against the rooster themed wallpaper. He always spoke to my pulse points. He never called me *Snow*.

The Beast did.

Snow, our unofficial safe word—a single syllable of a nickname tenderized my heart. Each letter a mallet swing. He couldn't take anymore. He reached his limit of me. The nickname put me back in my place. Locked us both back into character.

"We had a good day yesterday." Hudson said to the cock on the wall as he distanced himself from me.

On autopilot, I began the three-hour drive home.

Hudson's passenger window remained lowered the whole drive. Mine stayed up because I didn't want to eat my hair. I had enough turbulence. I didn't need the wind.

Hudson didn't say a word. I didn't either, but I was used to silence. I spent most of my life in some form of solitary confinement. Hudson lived the opposite lifestyle—he did everything he could not to be alone. When we were together, we stayed in public. If we hid away, it was in packed buildings. Most of the time we fucked in stairwells and dark corners. We had no shame in our voyeurism. We were secluded in our own little world—a snow globe that shook when he was around, sending magical glitter swirling. No one could get through the glass. No one could reach us. There was an *Us*. Fuck everyone else, they didn't exist.

I looked over at him, his eyes were closed. The wind blew through his hair. The sun set behind him. I once thought he was *my* lion. But our snow globe was busted, water leaked everywhere. Comparatively to a fishbowl, I didn't notice the water level until I was gulping oxygen and snatching handfuls of glitter—hoarding magic while my lungs deflated. Without enough surface area for diffusion, I couldn't accept oxygen. I couldn't survive in our snow globe. I had to go back to reality. *The Beast wanted to kill me.*

The low fuel sensor dinged in my car and Hudson's eyes snapped open. His gold stare landed on me and I looked away like he caught me. My face burned.

"I need to get gas," I said even though the sensor, gas station we pulled into, and right turn signal should have made it obvious. At the pump I thought about the last thing Hudson said to me before we shut each other out, *we had a good day yesterday.*

His perception of yesterday and mine were skewed, like he

buttoned his shirt correctly in the morning and I didn't, and no one corrected me. I felt the draft at my gut the whole day and couldn't understand it.

I heard once on daytime television that you think seven times faster than you speak. The average person speaks at approximately one hundred and fifteen words-per-minute, while you think at approximately eight hundred and twenty-five words-per-minute. His comment ran almost one hundred and thirty-eight times a minute as it mixed into my other thoughts, and it took me around five minutes to fill my tank. *How many times did his words embed in my brain?*

When I got back in the car, I took out my phone and did the math. 690. Hudson looked over at my math. It read 069 to him.

"One hundred and thirty-eight times five is six hundred and ninety." I said and put my car in drive. Hudson said, "Okay," and passed me a bag of chocolate-covered pretzels. He didn't ask questions because the math was right. I took a handful of pretzels and ate them one by one. I ate each pretzel like I was destroying bridges, one beam at a time. Outside bites before inside cross beams. It was one of my rules.

Hudson drank water and ate trail mix. He gave me every orange and green M&M because he also understood my rules. It was a silent transaction.

Yesterday Hudson laughed and smiled. He wore his excitement like a child. We swatted at each other like a couple of kids crushing hard. We played a supernatural version of the basketball game *Horse*. Except the word was Pony because I only thought of four categories. We took shots and competed. Hudson won strength, vision, speed, and hearing. I added a fifth category in true sore loser etiquette, fire. I handwrote fire at the bottom of our score sheet. Normally my cursive script looked like it belonged in the 1800s. On the score sheet it looked like a serial killer wrote it. The *F* came in hot and heavy. The *I* looked like an *e*, there was no dot to distinguish it. *R* was forgotten about, it looked more like the crest to the *e* which was over-looped and looked like an *L*. I won *Fel*.

We spent the first night by the campfire. Pinprick stars filled the black velvet sky above us. We've never been *that* alone before. Normally, there was a not too silent individual around us. Walls were thin, and we had supernatural hearing. Each wall to my apartment was its own soap opera. Except for the neighbors below us were Spanish, so we called their 'channel' a novella.

A part of me missed the noise—the 'channels' and distractions. In an Adirondack chair, I sat with Hudson by my side. A fire flickered at our feet. My thoughts were warm and fuzzy as I watched the flames belly dance. I smiled with a whimsical high.

Then I turned and noticed first that Hudson was white-knuckling his chair—followed by his darkened eyes and clenched teeth. His demeanor was feral, like a hungry wolf left out in the cold. While I fed my demons, he battled his.

Side by side, yet we lived such different lives. We were a part of the same scene and while I looked at the light, Hudson was trapped in the darkness.

16

HELLO GENEVIEVE

THE LOCKS WEREN'T CHANGED. My key fits and turns smoothly.

"Hello?" I ask and I shut the door behind me.

"In here," Genevieve says from within her bedroom. I follow her voice and find my roommate in her bed. Her appearance is better than the last time I saw her at the hospital. Less red, black and blue. More pink cast, black-winged eyeliner and yellowing bruises.

"I wasn't expecting to see you," Genevieve says as I cautiously enter. The swelling decreased in her face; there are still bandages around her nose and neck. Her right foot is propped up on a pillow with a shocking pink cast. The pink cast camouflaged with the walls and bedding, I almost sat on it. If it wasn't for Genevieve's sharp intake of breath, I would have.

"Why would you say that?" I sit down closer to the edge of the bed. My hands are empty and void of usefulness. I didn't bring anything. *I should have brought something.* White roses... Something not pink.

"It's been two weeks." There's a sneer in Genevieve's voice that perturbs me.

"I checked in on you through Ramona," I say as if it's any

conciliation. My half-ass attempt at friendship is at least an attempt. I haven't heard from her once. *Has she kept track of that?*

Too many questions busy themselves like bees in my mind. Each comment swarms and stings leaving poison behind. *Is the bruise between your shoulder blades still there from the initial kick? Did Hudson really say nothing while he was attacking you? Did you really not look behind you? Did you really not see his face? Why didn't you fight back?*

Paralyzed by the amount of information I want to learn, the question I ask is, "How are you?" My voice comes out tight and cracked. I feel onstage behind the podium about to give a presentation; my warm-up questions and icebreakers were not a hit. I lock up. I may pass out.

Genevieve doesn't respond—she rolls her eyes and gestures down her body.

Right, she has a skull fracture, multiple fractures to her left and right ribs, a broken right forearm and a sprained left ankle and internal injuries.

This isn't a great start.

"Listen, I don't mean to upset you," I say feeling off the stage and more like I'm breaking up with her and asking her out on a date at the same time.

The greenish tint to her bruising gives Genevieve a sickly pallor. "I'm tired Aviana." She turns the television off. Fashion magazines stack where a lover or partner's head would rest—the pillow is creased with their rectangular shape. The magazines have been there awhile.

A collection of pain medications is on her nightstand. The orange bottles hold the worst gateway drugs.

Everything in front of me is repulsive.

Genevieve takes a fashion magazine and drops it in her lap. The cover model is in all white. Red print types across the model's legs in bold, celebratory print: WHITE-HOT HOLIDAYS.

Genevieve won't look at me. We're both staring at the magazine, repulsed with the other. We can't acknowledge the physical pain a memory creates—or a face signifies. How it hurts her to look at me. All we see when we look at each other is him. *Hudson*. And what *he* did. How *he* beat her—and how *I* brought him into our lives.

"Didn't you read the police report?" Genevieve asks in a tone that insinuates I need to stop kicking the dead horse. The issue is dead. Hudson is dead. Fucking give it a rest.

"I did."

"Do you not believe me?"

"I do."

"Then why are you looking at me like you don't understand. You were there. You picked me up. You took me to the hospital. What more do you want to know?"

"I picked you up, but I wasn't there Genevieve. I WASN'T FUCKING THERE."

"But you're here now. And you see me. I'M RIGHT FUCKING HERE."

I get off the bed and kneel down on the carpet. Taking her small bandaged hand in mine, I press my forehead against her skin. It's been such a long time since I've been to church.

I breathe in her scent and take in her grace. Faith is about believing, even when science makes believing complicated to understand. I have faith in her. I believe her.

I look at her and I easily see the abuse take place. *It's all I see.*

Hudson warned me he's dangerous. Hudson told me he wanted to kill me. He isn't the boy who cried wolf. He is the wolf. He's the Beast he claimed himself to be the whole fucking time. I never thought he would kill me through someone else.

He set into motion psychological warfare and now I die a thousand deaths.

"My truth is my truth, what more do you want from me?" Genevieve asks. The style magazine in her lap shows the latest trends in glossy pages. The models are all dressed up with everywhere to go. Advice columns explain the operations on how to buy the best gift for your man. Genevieve doesn't read any of the words, only skims at the pictures.

I listen to the gratifying sound of a page turn. It's been a while since I've heard a page turn. Crisp like a dry leaf. I haven't been to the library since Hudson disappeared. I read online, on a tablet or app. I miss the touch of pages. I miss the weight of books. There is a sense of accomplishment with each page turn. The weight of a book slowly progressing from my right hand to my left until it eventually reaches *The End*. An electronic page 'curl' is just a gimmick that leaves me feeling cheap and deflated like a prostitute.

Genevieve turns the page aggressively. Her fingers separate and hold the next page like a writing utensil—still, poised, ready for direction.

"Have you ever taken a moment to wonder how the cabin caught on fire? The plumbing, gas, and electric weren't turned on. There was only one lantern that was battery operated. The closest neighbor was miles away, and even they were out of town." Genevieve says. "You spend so much time analyzing about Hudson that you dismiss the fire." Her thumb caresses the corner of the page, "When the officer first asked me about it, I thought he was trying to catch me in a lie. He had to show me photos on his phone for me to believe him. And as I swiped, I looked at the destruction and smiled hoping Hudson was part of the ashes. I wish I could have seen the fire." Her right hand slides up and down the page. From the top corner back down to the bottom. "You know, unlike floods or hurricanes that leave a mess, fires destroy and leave nothing behind." Her hand stops in the middle and says, "It would have been beautiful to see." She turns the page, her thought complete.

"He left me at the front of the cabin. He kicked me and stomped on me until I made it to the front door. Parts of my memory are redacted, and honestly, I'm happy about that. I may not remember seeing his face, but I wake up every morning and see mine. There's no alternate story here Aviana. Your boyfriend beat the fuck out of me and he's either dead or on the run."

Flip, skim and flip. "I remember his boots. His boots I fucking remember. I hope he's dead." Flip, flip, flip, she shuffles through the pages not even bothering with the images. "He's a fucking predator. He could have killed me. He could have killed you. I saved you from him." Genevieve craves movement. In her mind, she's on the run. I'm triggering her and she's back at the scene. Back to the abuse.

I place my hand on top of the magazine and stop the flipping out, "What can I do for you? How can I make this right?" *How can I erase him from your life?*

She pulls the magazine out from under my hand and tosses it to the floor, "I'm tired Aviana, let's have this heart-to-heart another day."

"Sure, that's fine," I stand up and say, "I'm going to grab some clothes and I'll be out of your hair."

"What clothes?" She yawns. "You had your new girlfriend Tracy clean up your room last week."

"Say what now?"

"Tracy, the little redhead that pranced around with three gorillas and emptied out the room in one night."

I run into the doorframe on my turn into *my* room. Or what I thought was *my* room, now the room holds a sleeping giant and all of his belongings. All of his *things*. The mattress he sleeps on rests directly on the floor in the darkest corner. My dresser is replaced with a wall of black wire racking—a preschool wall of cubbies for a giant man that stirs at my interruption.

A throne with its back to the windows. His domain is a sea of HD screens. Multiple monitors form a wall that blocks out any natural light.

Boxes reign haphazardly.

The giant does a double-take and looks at me oddly. *What am I doing in his room?*

"What do you want?" He asks. His blonde bed-head and rugged shadowed face makes him look like Adonis.

I step inside the room and shut the door. The giant sits upright revealing his chest and washboard abs. I wonder if he's naked beneath the sheet.

"This used to be my room." I say with my back against the door. He's beautiful. A Greek god from a painting or sculpture. Someone created him, he didn't do this on his own.

"So, you're Aviana?" He asks with a voice that could command Angels, or rather a roomful of women that either had tattooed angel wings or are named Angel—explains Genevieve.

"I am." I walk closer and sit down on the floor by the mattress. Up close, his likeness to Genevieve is unsettling. Her vanity has no boundaries. She found a way to fuck herself—incest, brother and sister boning to maintain the royal bloodline.

My hands sweat around each other. "Will you tell me about the move in and move out?"

He pulls his cell phone from under his pillow. The screen lights up. He grimaces, upset by the time. "I don't owe you an explanation. You've done a lot of damage." His hand massages the back of his neck. After an aggravated sigh he asks, "Why haven't you visited since the accident?"

"Accident? Is that what she calls it?" I ask and wake my phone up. It's two in the afternoon.

"Would you rather me use attack? Why haven't you stopped

by?" He asks again, intent on finishing this conversation. I woke him up, we're getting through this.

My fear rises—a cresting wave in front of a thalassophia inflicted individual.

"Do you have any fears Giant?" I ask watching the horizons of mine.

"My name's Mark."

"Mark?" I ask wringing my hands in safety knots.

"Yes, Mark."

"I prefer Giant. How tall are you?"

"6'4. Why is this the first time I'm seeing you? I don't want to ask again." His words barrel towards me.

"What happens if you ask again?" I ask and see the break.

"Lady..."

"My name's Aviana"

"Yeah, my name's Mark." The top curls and we're pulled in the pocket next to the breaking point.

"Hudson desecrated my temple." I say on the wave's shoulder.

"What?"

"Hudson broke what I held precious and took my sacred. I couldn't face my fears. I couldn't face her face."

Maritime conditions suddenly change, "Did you ever think of Genevieve? She was alone. A fucking cab dropped her off from the hospital."

"How do you know?" I ask trying to swim sideways through his riptide.

"I was hired as a singing telegram in this building. Genevieve got on the same elevator as me."

"Thank you for helping my friend," I say drowning.

"You should have been there. She still has night terrors. They aren't as often as they used to be, but she's still locked in that night."

"You're right." I sank.

I VISIT Genevieve and Giant the next day. White roses, soups and salads come with me. Giant does surveillance, he opens the door and checks my bags. I continue to call him Giant to his face. He only refers to me as Lady. Our banter helps distract Genevieve and lighten her mood. Her greenish tint grows rosier and begins to glow with each eye roll she gives us.

"Are you planning on moving back in?" Giant asks me in bed. Genevieve hums softly between us. I brush her soft pale hair between my fingers. We've spent the day in bed watching Disney movies and getting high. I'm the only smoker, the other two ate edibles. It's nice, a single day vacation. If I didn't look at Genevieve, I could almost forget all the trauma.

"No, I never moved out remember?"

"Right, the ever-elusive Tracy came and stole all your things." Giant says with a giggle. The gorgeous man giggles.

"You're not funny."

"Actually he is. Now both of you leave, you're too loud. I'm going to take a nap." Genevieve whines, pops a pain pill past her full-chapped lips and swallows the drugs down with a drink of water.

Giant and I get out of bed and make our way to the living room where he takes the controller and turns the television on to a basketball game. I watch the ball dribble back and forth in a zoned-out haze.

"Why don't you play basketball?" I ask him during a commercial break.

"I'm too pretty and I don't play with balls."

"Do you model?" I ask as a 4x4 Chevy pickup drives a snow-plow through a commercial. Christmas trees are loaded in the bed.

"I'm an actor."

The game returns with chants and hoots. Sneakers squeak

on the polished floor. "What have you been in?"

"A few local projects and commercials."

"You're still just a pretty face?"

"Who invited you here?" He asks like I'm a scoundrel.

"I live here."

"The fuck you do." He says and tosses a pillow at me.

Halftime buzzes in at eleven at night. The red team is beating the blue. Giant looks over at me, we are on opposite sides of the couch. Both of us are absently scrolling through our social media feeds, the game in the background.

"It's getting late Lady. Do you need me to give you a ride home?"

"Home?" I snark, "What home?" Before he can respond I say, "You mean with Tracy at the end of a rainbow?"

"No, she moved to a house made of candy. She rents from a haggard witch that eats children."

"Is that where my things are? At the corner of 'fuck me sideways' and 'I hate you'. I know the place."

"Good, if not, I know how to get there. I moved you after all."

"Did you really help move all my stuff out?"

Giant laughs and puts his phone down, "I did."

I put my phone down too, "Then you know where my things are?"

"No, I just moved everything into a U-Haul."

"You know there's a huge part of me that thinks Genevieve had everything moved or sold out of anger."

"Then why aren't you more upset?"

"I'm still numb, I'm not sure how to respond. I don't even know where to sleep at night. Do I stay here and crash on the couch of my battered best friend who now has a live-in roommate? Or do I continue to stay in," I look over at Giant and he gives me the stink eye, daring me to say Hudson's name. "Or", I continue, "do I stay in Ben's guest room with the ex-girlfriend? I'm not crashing at Ramona's."

"I'll be your third option." He says with a cheeky smile.

"Aren't you fucking Genevieve?"

"I'm a great cuddler, no one said anything about fucking."

I curl into the couch and debate just crashing on the spot.

"Where are you paying rent?" Giant asks.

"Neither location."

He turns the television off giving me his full attention. "You never paid rent here?"

"No, Genevieve has a sugar-daddy for rent."

His head turns incredulously. "That hussy makes me pay rent. I thought I was getting a deal."

I laugh and sit upright, "I think I'll take you up on that drive. I don't think this couch will fix the gaping hole I have in my life."

"No, I don't believe it will," Giant says. I check in on Genevieve and she is still sleeping.

In the car, I think about Genevieve and all her injuries and their physical manifestations. Streetlights periodically shine through the window illuminating my white skin for fractions of a second. No cuts or fading scars line my arms.

I wish my inner turmoil released—leak out my veins. I carry my pain with me where no one can see it. Its existence only lies within me. There are no supporting muscles or limbs to help take the weight and pressure off. The only support system I have are my friends and even those are negligible.

"Are we friends Giant?" I ask.

Giant turns right on Evansville Drive. "I don't see why we can't be."

Jokingly he adds, "Just don't have any of your future boyfriends try to kill me."

My hand is on the door handle before he puts the car in park.

"That was too soon, I'm sorry. I was trying to make you laugh." He says with his foot on the break.

"Harr Harr."

"I know you didn't sick your boyfriend on Genevieve."

I wince and pull on the handle to open the door. Giant's hand lands on my shoulder before I leave, "I'm sorry Lady, I know you lost your boyfriend and almost lost your best friend." His hand on my shoulder squeezes in comfort.

"They were together at most three hours and those three hours created such a ripple effect that I can't see over the waves."

Another soft squeeze to my shoulder. "Give it more time."

"Ugh, I hate that phrase. It's too passive."

"Time will give you more perspective-"

I interrupt, "More perspective on how murderous Hudson was?"

Giant removes his comforting hand, "Don't say his name."

A moment passes, and a man walks by with his teacup yorkie. It barks at us in the car. The owner's shoe size is larger than their dog. He tries to scold the yorkie as they walk away. The yorkie wags their stubby butt excited for the attention, even if negative.

"I already feel like I'm not an active participant in my life. Shit keeps happening and all I can say is, *'oh, so we're doing this now, ok.'* But how do I keep saying that? How do I just roll with this flow when everything goes against my current?"

"Maybe you should talk to your therapist friend more. She might give you more coping tools."

"No thanks, I'd rather live with Tracy in the candy house," I say and get out.

"Everything will be alright Lady."

"Right, right, just give it time," I say and Giant gives me a megawatt smile.

"Do you think he kicked her because he ran out of socially acceptable ways to express himself? He ran out of words and resorted to tantrums?"

Giant's smile fades, "Too soon Lady, too soon."

HEALING STONES AND THE WORDS
WE THROW

Two MONTHS after Hudson's disappearance—and it's like he never existed. I haven't spoken his name out loud in weeks.

Terra flutters around Ben's house with a phone attached to her as if it were a cochlear implant. When she's still, she's merely perching on the steps, at the edge of a couch cushion, one ass-cheek on a stool with her computer teetering on her knees. She's ready and waiting for her phone or computer to chime. Then she's off and her fingers are flying against the keyboard—a true millennial with fingers that type over sixty words-per-minute.

At night I stalk her and eavesdrop on her conversations. Keep your friends close and your enemies' closer mentality.

Last night she had two girl friends over. I couldn't remember their names if you paid me. Jennifer, Jamie, Jackie, Jessica? Both were J names, and both were overly common and easily forgettable. What struck me was when one J got up and went to the restroom, I heard the other J being catty with Terra. "Do you think she's pregnant? That's like the fourth time she's peed."

Terra looked in the direction of the bathroom and shook her head offended she didn't pick up on the pregnancy first. I stood in the corner offended that J's vagina was being discussed so openly. *When did it become socially acceptable to ask women when and if they are going to be pregnant? What if she had a miscarriage? What if she delivered a stillborn? What if she didn't want babies, and she just gained weight?*

J's wedding ring was a beacon for questions pertaining to her vagina. *Are you trying? How many do you want? Why aren't you pregnant? Better get that bun in the oven, times-a-ticking. Having babies is the next step in life.* All those questions and comments were tossed to J when she returned, it made me nauseous. So much so that I had to smoke a 'j' to hold the bile down. Their conversation made me feel less than human because I wasn't sure if I wanted a baby. I felt every bit sterile and mutated.

I wanted to yell that J was raped and was having the rapist's baby. I wanted to yell something fucked up to stop the invasion of privacy. J's into bestiality, who knows what will come out of her who-ha—maybe a centaur, minotaur or harpy. Take it easy Other J.

I ashed my joint and decided to call Other J, OJ for her conspiring tendencies. The glove fit.

J wasn't pregnant, but she was trying. They all crossed their fingers and cheers'd with wine. Not sure how drinking would benefit, but I was spying and couldn't share my opinion. If I could interject I'd ask if there was a male equivalent to the '*are you pregnant*' question. *Are men asked if they're pregnant? After having children do men get asked if they're having vasectomies as brazenly?*

If a couple doesn't physically hold a baby, then they aren't pregnant. Case closed. Don't get stuck asking an overweight gal if she's preggers. It's a guaranteed bad time.

Today Terra scrolls through healing crystals on her computer. Head tilted to the left, her shoulder props her phone up to her ear. Her right hand writes while her left hand continues to scroll.

"Right, medium veggie." She says stopping on an image of clear quartz. She reads the fine print and continues her pizza order. "Well-done please with a side of ranch."

I pull my phone out and pretend I'm texting, or otherwise occupied. I pass Terra. My phone is turned off and dead, I'm only smudging my oily fingerprints all over my screen. It appears like I'm playing a game. One I'm winning.

"Delivery." She says and doesn't acknowledge me. I don't acknowledge her either. This is how we survive.

Ben is never at the house. He's getting it *in* at the gym or getting it *in* between whoever's legs can spread out the fastest. The last time I saw him I asked if he wanted me to pay rent.

"You don't need to worry about it Aviana." He slung his gym bag over his shoulder. "Hudson kept most of his money in the gun safe in the basement. He said if he ever disappeared it was the house's money. I consider you and Terra house expenses."

"Did you ever ask why he thought he would disappear?" I asked watching him walk away.

At the front door he turned back and said, "No, he's disappeared before." The door shut, and I felt it push me back.

AT A DIFFERENT DOOR with golden numbers, I close it softly behind me.

Genevieve and I have been fighting over Tracy. I'm convinced Genevieve gave my property away.

I feel a rise of anger that I'm finally entitled too. This anger is mine. Pure unadulterated anger. Every other emotion of mine is layered and soaked deep in shame, confusion, and betrayal. Anger I can wring out of me like a sponge.

"I don't know a Tracy." I say to Giant and Genevieve. They are both sitting on the couch. Genevieve is painting Giant's fingernails aquamarine. She paints his ring finger black. I pull my phone out of my back pocket and pause with my contacts on the screen.

"Why do you paint the ring finger a different color?" I ask Genevieve.

"Femme-flagging. Other ladies need to know I'm into ladies." Giant says looking through glitter topcoat options.

Genevieve dips the nail polish brush back into the glass jar. "It's an accent nail to give a pop of color. You want your nails done next?"

I look down at my chewed-up nails. "No thanks." I sit down next to Genevieve and scroll through the M's of my contacts to the K's.

People whose names I don't want to remember I enter in my phone as Katie. If I only know you because I sell you weed, I enter you as Katie and put a 'w' word in the notes or use a 'W' last name.

As long as you know who I am, I don't need to remember who Katie Wednesday is—they'll find me when I walk in a room and I'll be awkward and not say your name. But I'd be awkward and not remember your name even if I tried. I'm just awkward. This method provides less stress. Keeps buyers at a distance. It's another one of my rules.

Finally, to the T's in my contacts, there are only four names; Theresa, Teresa, Travis and Taylor. No Tracy. I show my evidence.

"'Tracy could be a Katie." Genevieve says applying a silver glitter topcoat to Giant's ring finger.

"If I was dating her I would put her name in my phone." I scroll back up to the G's so she could see her name: Goodness Genevieve. Giant takes my phone and enters in his information one-handed. When he hands it back I see a name above Goodness Genevieve, Giant Dick Mark. I click the edit screen and copy, cut and paste 'Dick Mark' into the notes, leaving Giant as his contact name.

"You could have changed her name to prove a point," Genevieve says. Giant blows on his nails.

"But I didn't."

"Okay," Genevieve says not believing me, only appeasing me. She leans back into the couch with a nail file.

"Why'd you give my things to a stranger?" I ask annoyed with the scrapping of her nail file. The sound might as well be nails screeching across a chalkboard.

Genevieve continues to file her already squared off nails. "Because she asked for them."

"Shouldn't you have checked with me first? I was only a call away."

"Exactly, you were only a call away. Why didn't you ever check on me?"

"I did-"

"THROUGH SOMEONE ELSE!" She interrupts.

"I explained and apologized A THOUSAND TIMES OVER."

Once our voices rise, Giant throws me over his shoulder and escorts me out the door. He says his same worn-out catch phrases.

"Give her more time." He says.

"There's nothing you can do about it now." He says.

"Keep positive, it's only material objects. Everything can be replaced." He says.

I follow up with a string of fucks that include "Fuck time", "Fuck you," and the ever consistent "Fuck your logic." At times I'd wave my hand around like I had a magical wand and Giant would disappear. Other times I try to barrel through him to continue my screaming match with Genevieve.

Honestly, it isn't even about my things. Well, it is, and it isn't. Most of my belongings came from thrift stores. None of them held a nostalgic memory. What raises my blood pressure is how easily she dismisses me.

When I verbalize this to Giant, he tells me to reverse my perspective and see that Genevieve felt dismissed by me as well.

"Fuck your logic," I say and weasel my way back in to give my one-thousandth and one apology.

Yet the apology train isn't reciprocated.

When I leave I stutter step because it dawns on me that Genevieve redirects each of our fights back to me being in the wrong and her being the victim. I'm still nowhere closer to finding out who Tracy is and how she found out where I stored my belongings. It has to be an inside job.

AT THE THRIFT STORE, I purchase yet another bag of random clothing I shouldn't have to buy. On my walk home I watch the sunset between buildings. The night soaks into my pores and takes root in my darkness. I am light on my feet when I turn the corner onto Evansville Drive. I see a white van pull away from the curb. The white paint is a dirty gray in the dull streetlight. The van drives away before I can read any logo on its side. The back window instructs: WASH ME.

Ben is on the other side of the door when I open it. I run directly into him dropping my bag of oversized ugly sweaters and worn t-shirts.

"Av, you just missed her." He says reaching for the door and then deciding against it. He doesn't have super speed, there is no way for him to catch a moving vehicle. For a couple seconds when he lurched for the door he thought he could, and a small frown breaches his lips in disappointment. I almost want to tell him I might. However, if I did, my cover would be blown and as Ricky Ricardo would say, *I'd have some explainin' to do.*

"The van was for me? A delivery?" I ask heeling off my sneakers. The backs fold inwards, their integrity shot.

"Tracy stopped by. She was looking for you. I tried to call." Ben says walking away from me and to the stairs.

I pull my phone out of my pocket. Then drop it with the adrenaline rushing through me. I juggle my phone like a hot potato before I clutch it and see three missed calls from Ben. I stare at my phone and expect to see Tracy's name and number appear. It doesn't. It still reads Ben. Three separate times.

"Ben you called me three times."

"I know, I'm the one that fucking called. Why didn't you answer?" He asks with a foot on the first step.

"Because I was working..." I shake my phone like it's an eight ball and a different script will appear.

"Then I visited Genevieve..." *Outlook is not so good.*

"Then I went to the thrift store." *Very doubtful.*

Ben steps off the step giving me his full attention again. "You're visiting Genevieve?"

"Yeah, I visit a couple of times a week. I thought I told you." I shut my phone down, it's no good to me.

"No, you haven't, how is she?" I definitely did. I went there often, even if Ben and I passed like two ships in the night, we still gave the customary single sentence updates.

"Less beat the fuck up, now tell me why Tracy visited." He makes a face like he's sucking on a lemon and turns back to the stairs, "She was just looking for you. Said she's your friend from high school-"

"High School? I didn't go to fucking high school." I was under surveillance as a science project at the time. "I was home-schooled," I say to help correct the confused expression on Ben's face.

"Oh, well, either way, she was looking for you. Said she'd stop by another night." He takes another step up the stairs and away from me.

"Did she take anything of mine?"

"What? No. Why would she take anything?"

My hands rise in praise; hallelujah someone agrees with me. "EXACTLY! Why would she!?"

His hand grips the railing like its physical sanity.

I lower my hands, "Sorry, continue."

"That was it. She asked for you, you weren't here, I tried to call and you didn't answer, so she left."

"She left in the pedophile van?"

"She did."

"Alone?"

"Yes?" He says like he's questioning me now.

"No love note? She didn't ask for my phone number or take my things?"

"Again, why is she taking your things?"

"I DON'T KNOW! But she's done it before."

"So, you know her?"

"No, I don't know her."

"What is happening?" Ben looks for a witness. His eyes fixate on the red ceramic deer on the mantle and they exchange a look.

"EXACTLY!" I screech because I've been wondering what the fuck's been happening for weeks.

"STOP YELLING AT ME! I'M JUST THE MESSENGER!"

"WHY IS EVERYONE YELLING?" Terra hollers from the upstairs hallway. She moves to the railing and looks down at me like I'm her Romeo and she's my Juliet.

"Av had a visitor," Ben says from the bottom of the stairs. If our lines connected, we'd make an acute triangle.

"Oh, was is it the redhead?"

"You know her?" I ask.

"She stopped by a few days ago, left a cryptic message about meeting in the woods? Hold on, I'll get the note." Terra turns away and walks as slowly as humanly possible out of eyesight. I barge pass Ben quicker than humanly possible. Ben's against the wall with his hands up pleading innocence. I snatch the note from Terra with greedy hands to unveil a plain white piece of paper with the words: meet me in the woods. I turn the page over and it's blank. I look up at Terra with a blank expression that she matches. I look down at Ben and he wears the same blank expression. He's looking at the stag again for guidance. We're all wearing a deer in headlights expression. If we connected our lines now we'd be Aries, the Ram constellation. The stag as the ass-end, Ben as Hamal, me as Sheratan and Terra as Mesarthim.

"Meet me in the woods," I say hoping it might unlock a magical hidden text. It doesn't. I walk slowly down the stairs repeating the phrase and enunciating different syllables. Showing my teeth and keeping my tongue forward and down I say slowly, "meet me IN the woods."

"Where are you going?" Ben asks as I pass him.

"To da wooDs." I say sounding like hooked on phonics didn't work for me—or ET trying to phone home and no one accepted my collect call. Pay-phones don't exist anymore.

———

Four days later with chilled hands on a local map, I wipe my nose across my sleeve. A clear snot trail darkens the fabric. I caught a cold aimlessly wandering the woods looking for smoke signals and red hair. No telltale tracks or markings were left behind.

Maybe I'm in the wrong woods. I scan my map and begin making notes and plotting a course to visit all the wooded areas in a fifty-mile radius. While I'm circling a set of woods nestled into the suburbs, the chair next to me squeaks out.

I look to my right and see Giant. "What the fuck are you doing here?" I ask. My black marker circles another batch of promising woods.

"I'm supposed to be a buffer." He says with his elbows on the table not looking at me. We're at the kitchen table that seats eight. Six empty chairs are his audience.

Only partially listening to him I ask, "Why are you telling me you're a fluffer?"

He pulls the marker from my hand and the black ink presses into my palm as I try to keep my tool.

"Aviana," he says my full first name in a scolding tone. "You know I'm an outsider, but I'm dragging myself in. I need you on my side."

"The grass isn't greener in these parts. Stay on your side of the fence." I say still staring at my map, wishing for my marker and mentally drawing circles and lines.

The chair across from Giant pulls out and Ramona takes a seat. She looks adoringly at Giant. Ben filters through and takes a seat beside Ramona. He looks at Ramona and follows her gaze, Giant's a new golden retriever and he's a Chinese crested with a bad haircut. His body falls heavily in his seat and he elbows Ramona.

"Let's wait for Terra and Genevieve," Ramona says to Ben while eyeing Giant out of the corner of her eye.

"Giant should I be drinking for this?" I whisper.

Ramona has her listening ears on and asks, "Why do you call him Giant?"

I look at him and look at her, his nickname should be obvious.

I get up and grab the Jack Daniels bottle and a can of coke. It's going to be me or Jack as the last one standing. Terra and Genevieve are in their prospective seats when I return. Genevieve next to Giant and Terra at the head of the table between Genevieve and Ben. No one sits across from me, or to my left.

"Genevieve, do you want to tell everyone why we are here?"

Ramona prompts. She looks at Giant for approval and he winks at her.

"I've decided to drop my charges against Huds-" Genevieve begins to say Hudson's name, then stops at Giant's cough. He has a serious aversion to Hudson's name. Terra does a quiet golf clap at the news. Ben scratches his head but is still more perturbed over Ramona's attraction to Giant. I screw off and remove Jack's cap and take a long pull followed by a coke chaser. My eyes are watering and I'm coughing, but I'm listening to every word now.

"Without Genevieve, there is no evidence that-" Terra stops and looks at Giant before saying Hudson's name. She pauses and rephrases, "The evidence is that he bought the cabin and his vehicle was on the premises. But the cabin burned, why would he burn his own property?"

"I don't think he started the fire," I say and have another mouth to mouth with Jack.

"I don't think so either. There's no motive. This whole case lacks causation. The only communication they had was over you." Terra says indicating me to the jury of Ben, Ramona, and Giant.

"There is no direct evidence, merely circumstantial. The only witness is Genevieve and if she cannot place... The prosecution's evidence is that they were both present at the scene. Simply present." *Dundun.* Terra concludes, confirming she's watched an immense amount of Law and Order.

"Sounds like you have it all figured out," Giant says and takes Genevieve's hand in his. He runs his thumb back and forth in a comforting gesture.

"I just want this all to be over with," Genevieve says.

Ramona reaches across the table and puts her hand on top of Giant's hand, "You're not alone."

It's unclear who she's trying to comfort. I hold Jack's neck. I won't let him go. This isn't the Titanic.

"So there's no justice? —Hudson runs away without giving an explanation and we just forget it all happened? " Ben asks Giant as if this were a conversation *between men*.

Giant removes his hand from being sandwiched and crosses his arms. I nudge Jack over to give Giant a version of my comfort.

"He leaves. Again." Ben says now looking at Terra, if anyone should be offended it's them. This is now Hudson's second disappearing act.

"He needs help, not a prison." Terra defends looking at Ramona for psychological backing. I take Jack back and make out with him for a minute while Ramona acts as an expert witness. I belch and confess that I started the fire, but no one hears me except Giant. He stares at me like I grew horns and wings. I tap my head with my vision blurring. No horns.

"We still need to find Hudson." Ben reiterates. Giant gets up and takes Jack with him. I get up and follow because Jack is my ride.

Outside in the chilly temperatures, I sit on the back stoop.

"Have you been following the case at all?" Giant asks. I shake my head and hiccup.

"The Judge that originally signed off on all the warrants and legal bullshit was found mentally incompetent. He's had a rapidly forming brain tumor in his frontal lobe that put all his cases in jeopardy. Everything he's touched has grounds for being inadmissible because he wasn't of sound mind." Giant talks and paces. "For fuck's sake, he tried to pick his ten-year-old son up from school butt-ass naked. I mean what the fuck?! He had no idea he left the house with no clothes. He remembered to tie his shoes, but no clothes."

I slither down on the grass and lie flat on the cold surface. " I had no idea." The grass is stiff like over soaped carpet that wasn't rinsed. White with residual snow.

"This happened two days ago."

"I've been searching for Tracy."

"Seriously Aviana give it a rest, we know you know her."

"And how do we know this?"

"She knew things about you. Genevieve didn't just let her in the door. She asked her questions about what you looked like and random shit like what your favorite ice cream flavor is and she knew. She knew all the answers."

"It's chocolate chip," I say with chattering teeth. Giant looks at me and mumbles about going back inside to get a coat for me. I ask for Jack because I don't want to alone. My reasoning is sound and Giant slams the door going back inside.

I take a few swigs and the fire burns in my belly.

"We're going to find this redheaded bitch," I tell Jack. The old-time script on the bottle waves and I'm off down the road and into the woods. Tracy is the villain to my story and I'm ready to convict. I have tangible evidence; the note she left burns a hole in my pocket. I am Judge, jury, and executioner. I am woman. Hear me ROAR.

After stomping around and accusing shadows and branches I soften with Jack in my clutches. Trees sway and beckon. I pull heavy swallows from Jack and toast the night sky. I spin around trees singing in the metaphorical rain. I monkey around branches and lean against trunks and drink and sing. Sing and drink.

"Jack Jack Jack we're loo-ooooo-oking for a redhead." Leaves crush and crackle beneath my shoes. My lips chatter, my hiccup is strong. "And you kno-oh-oh-oh-ow what they say about redheads." My left arm around a tree trunk, I use the bottle as a microphone. "They're all fucking crazy-"

A twig snaps and it's not one of my twigs.

"Who goes there?" I spin in a circle. The gypsy trees turn into prison bars confining the air from my lungs. Jack leaves my clutches. Or I drop him. It's hard to tell with numb fingers.

A stranger emerges.

"Red?" I ask and momentarily look down at Jack. He's tipped over on his side. My liquid courage drains from his open mouth. A tear falls and freezes against my cheek because I let him down. This is the first time I've cried, and it's over a bottle of Jack. I'm the last one standing.

The stranger takes a step closer. I take one back.

My heart stops. "Red is that you?"

My breath comes out in short staccato bursts. The stranger reminds me of my kidnapper from when I was a kid—too dark and only solid to appease my mental stability. Though I'm not mentally stable and his reappearance is doing nothing but more damage.

My back is against a tree. Sap gets tangled in my hair. My fear spotlights the stranger. *Is this my kidnapper?* The edges of my vision fade with the lack of oxygen reaching my brain.

The stranger takes a step closer. Their body is over six feet tall. My heels dig into the tree bark. Shredded bark powders the roots. My vision goes wonky.

A small redheaded female unfolds from the branch above me. A handkerchief covers my nose and mouth and I become limp.

MY ROOM

BILE BUBBLES up and out of my mouth. I roll over and hurl all over a blue rug I've never seen before. My first thought is that I hate the blue color. Three tones of electric blue swirl across a shag rug. My second thought is that Jack is bound to leave a stain. My vomit is an abstract painting.

I'm overwhelmed with Jack. Jack is wafting out of my pores and up from the ghastly blue shag rug. My brain is falling out of my head. If I wasn't still drunk, I might have jumped up in alarm. But since this isn't my first rodeo at being stolen, I turn away from the shag carpet masterpiece and take in my surroundings.

Spider webs in the rafters blow out like sails. Wooden beams anchor a roof I've never seen before.

My eyes don't make it very far. They snag on the eighties composite wood nightstand. It's eerily too similar to the one Tracy stole. A plastic cup of water sits on its surface. A ring of condensation puddles at the base. Light shines out of a camper's lantern that sits on the outside corner of my nightstand. It's the only source of light. No windows, just a steady draft.

I toss my clunky hand above me and search the round curve

of the composite wood bedframe. I shimmy the headboard and hear the stripped bolts and headboard flex from too hard sex.

I sit up and drink some water and taste iron—well water.

All of my second-hand thrift store belongings surround me. My room from Genevieve's apartment is reconstructed in a dilapidated barn. Half the ceiling goes straight to the roof, the other is a loft that I can't see into. There's no TV or electronics. My cheap bookshelf holds more books than I originally owned. At least I'm not stuck in a bathtub in a shed with buckets. I'm afforded comforts.

I get up on woozy feet like a fawn on newfound legs. I wobble to what appears to be a telephone booth a lumberjack made. A crescent moon is cut out of the door. I walk inside and see a wooden plank with a hole cut out. This must be the outhouse. I piss in a hole and wipe with toilet paper. Thank god for toilet paper. I toss the tissue in the hole and feel environmentally friendly for not having to flush.

Even for a drunk, I'm handling this far too well. Maybe it's the sick sense of déjà vu of being stolen for the third time. Perhaps it's Jack's continued reappearance to my senses that has me distracted. Sour liquor continues to seep out of my pores. Jack's rancid taste is still in my mouth. I look back into the outhouse and see a small cubby with a plastic cup that holds antibacterial soap, a toothbrush, and toothpaste. I try to brush my teeth but my mouth is too dry. Gritty micro beads cover the inside of my mouth. Minty fresh with a Jack aftertaste.

I crawl back into bed and cocoon myself. My mind pitter-patters in circles. Three predominate letters lace through my thoughts in unison, W.H. Y? Followed shortly by the revolving complete thought: *What the fuck is happening?* The thought flips back and forth between tenses. *What the fuck happened? What the fuck will happen? What the fuck is happening?*

My musings peck like a woodpecker at my brain. *Peck, Peck,*

Peck. The gyrus and sulcus of my gray matter have gaping holes and craters. My hands can't keep my brain within my skull.

"Hello?" I whimper sounding like a scared little girl, which was not the intent. My voice cracks as I ask again.

"Hi!" Comes a cheerful voice from the upper loft.

A spinning red figure lands on the floor in front of me. Stepping away from my abstract art, a small curly-haired redhead with bright violet eyes and very pale skin lands by my bed. Freckles spray her cheeks like a firework display of melatonin occurred in utero.

Hands held high with wrists twisted out in perfect form, she waits for my acknowledgment.

"Hi?... Tracy? Where are we?" Residual weariness has my muscles and joints crying out with individual pulses, aching for a banana.

Tracy floats around the room like a delicate fairy. "I prepared a script. I prepared much for your arrival." She sneers on *your arrival*. A folded piece of paper is unfolded from her front pocket. She coughs as though clearing her throat at a microphone. Fist to mouth she makes a presentation before saying, "Aviana you are safe here. If you need anything you are to ask me. You are not to attempt to leave because you will not be able." Tracy then jumps and grabs hold of the wall and flips her way up the rafters. She's a Pixie-Leprechaun-Tarzan.

———

I STARE up at the rafters and wait. I watch the cobweb's sail billow by the draft. I'm no longer drunk, and my overwhelming emotions make me feel about to implode. I don't feel stolen like I once did. I feel properly kidnapped. In a strange way, I feel wanted. Selected by a stranger and drugged by a redhead.

Tracy hangs from the rafters swinging a tray in front of my face by a long rope. The sweet smell of freshly sliced melons, oranges, and waffles topped with whipped cream and maple syrup swings gently inches above my face.

Tracy lowers the tray. "Breakfast is served, mademoiselle." The metal touches my blanket-clad legs. Tracy ties off the rope to a beam and disappears in the loft. There is no natural light, I don't know if this is breakfast for breakfast, or breakfast for another meal.

Alone again I eat my 'breakfast' in peace. Loneliness becomes strangling after a few rounds of dropped down meals from the attic loft and silent conversations. There is no table talk. No table at all.

I felt alone in the shed, yet this level of loneliness is worse. Being in a room with someone and feeling alone is far, far worse. I'm looked at and not seen. I'm a checkmark off a to-do list. I'm inhabiting without cohabitating. I'm a body without a being.

Primarily I stick to my bed in a cocoon to keep warm from the draft. There are only two doors. One for the outhouse and the other is a bolted shut large sliding door. I've walked and touched every plank of wood I can reach. Splinters embed in my fingers and I watch them slowly work themselves out over the course of days. One day, two, five, eleven, four. The concept of time is only measured by the meals lowered from the rafters.

There's a small spigot, a bar of soap, and a washcloth between the outhouse and the barn wall. I take a whore's bath and wash my pits and vagina after every third meal. There's a small grate that I stand on. Cold well water is my only option. I miss hot water. I miss warmth.

On my nightstand, there are two books: The Count of Monte Cristo and The Executioner's Song. The packed books in the bookstand are all in foreign languages with no pictures. There are only two books I can read, and I've read them both cover to cover.

"What do you do when you aren't dropping from the rafters?" I ask Tracy.

"Planning my next descent," Tracy says as she plays along the beams of her personal jungle gym. She does this often. She won't initiate conversation, but she'll talk back to me like a parrot.

"Do you stay up there all the time?"

"Most of the time."

"You're allowed to leave?"

"At night."

"Why only at night?"

"Because it's not during the day."

"Does he know?" I ask trying to backdoor information from her. There has been no mention of the shadowed figure, but I saw them. I know I did. I may have been beyond coherence, but those last moments before Tracy drugged me were captured in a mental snapshot. The shadowed figure jarred a memory in me that triggered the snap, the shot, the recollection.

"He knows."

"Who's he?"

"He is who he is."

"Why do you let him tell you what you do?"

"He doesn't." Instantly angered Tracy swings her way back to the loft where she stays out of sight.

"Wait... when do I get out of this room?"

No response.

Eventually, the lantern burns out. The barn is steeped in darkness. Tracy tosses batteries at me to change out the lantern —but I don't. I don't eat and I stop bathing. I stop moving. I'm not living. I don't want the light.

The batteries fall off the bed and through the slot between

the headboard and mattress. They hit the wall and scatter into dust bunny burrows. Underneath my bed has never been cleaned. Nothing is clean.

Light is forced upon me. Tracy wraps battery-operated LED multicolor Christmas lights around the beams. The primary colored lights remain permanently on. Their glow is an optical illusion.

My internal circadian system is entirely fucked. I keep my eyes sealed tight and try to sleep. My mind won't turn off, it constantly stews and marinates over the shadowed figure. I compare and contrast my past abduction with my current one. One thought continues to bubble forth—a different shadow has stolen me. I'm being utilized not used. The rumination sticks.

The crock of shit I've cooked up keeps my thoughts churning and bubbling. Sleep is elusive. Outwardly I'm cata- tonic, inwardly I'm manic. My rigid muscles and bones squeak, pop and groan when I visit the outhouse. I drink water, seal my eyes closed, and only get up when my bladder fills like a balloon and threatens to burst.

I drink water.
Seal my eyes closed.
Get up and take a piss.

> Drink water.
> Eyes closed.
> Take a piss.

>> Water.
>> Closed.
>> Piss.

When Tracy lowers food, I roll away. The silver tray is left on my bed. The food and glasses never spill, I'm careful of that at first. My white down comforter remains white, even as a tablecloth.

After a few meals, I run out of room to roll and begin rolling into the food like a pig in a sty. Tracy resorts to tossing granola and protein bars down from the loft. The past few bars have hit my head. I don't feel them. I don't feel anything. My body is unresponsive. All my fuel is being distributed to the stew of my thoughts. The consistency is now of thick oil or tar—a viscous liquid that requires too much energy to churn. I don't even want to leave the dilapidated barn anymore. I simply don't want to be.

I think of death. Not suicide. I wonder about a peaceful death and how calming it would be to just slip away. My emotions aren't negative which should be troubling. But I'm untroubled. I know suicide is the most selfish act, yet when was the last time I did something for myself?

My comforter is pulled off me with all the food and fixings. A large clatter and turmoil ensue. This is the second time Tracy's been on the ground floor. I hear her wrapping the comforter up like a bindle. I shiver with the draft but keep my eyes sealed tight. The shiver alone is exhausting.

When I exit the outhouse scalding water is dumped on me from above. I only know it's scalding from the pink tint of my skin. A white bar of soap is tossed at my shoulder. It ricochets and skids on the floor like a hockey puck. My feet step in crusty Jack. Tracy never took my rug masterpiece. I wonder if she thought my vomit was a part of the pattern.

My shoulder hurts from the soap attack. There's no fat on my body. I'm skin and bones. An ugly groan slithers out of me when I crawl back in bed. My voice is hoarse from disuse.

I think of suicide notes and wonder how people find the words to say goodbye. I wouldn't know what to say. I'd have perpetual writer's block. *How do you say it's not you but me eloquently? Are these notes all written in numb shock? Am I in a numb shock? What am I? What's my fucking purpose?* I pause on that churn and circle back... *What's my fucking purpose? Why would someone kidnap me in order to let me stew?*

My hollow stomach howls touching my spine. The fact that nothing is happening constipates my mind. My mental stew is over stirred, overcooked, and hardening my synapses. Sparks stop firing. Thoughts stop emerging.

With sealed shut eyes I grab a granola bar and mindlessly chew. I add eating a granola bar a day to my routine. I don't want to die.

A clean comforter drifts across me. A reward for eating.

A few tears streak down my face. Warmth shouldn't be so groundbreaking. The salt of my tears drips between my lips. My succulent tears are over seasoned.

A calming touch wipes away another fat tear before it slides down the contours of my cheek. The knuckle belongs to a hand much larger than mine.

My eyes burst open and I shoot up banging my head. A pained sound erupts out of a man. The ugly grunt is all too familiar.

Hudson.

My eyes strain in the darkness. The Christmas lights are turned off. *How long have the Christmas lights been turned off?*

Fumbling, I try to switch everything near my fingers and forget that I didn't bother replacing the batteries in my lantern. Books and cups tumble and fall. I knock the lantern over in the process of searching for its switch, it breaks with a loud crash.

The room has never seemed as black. The lack of color isn't from the absence of color, but complete absorption. No light can reflect.

I stop my chaos and listen. The air is heavy with intent, a coming storm which quickly dissipates when I hear Tracy's voice, "Need some light?"

The Christmas lights are turned back on. Bright primary colors twinkle and strobe mockingly.

"Hudson was here... I swear he was here." I say and spin around. My cup spilled onto the blue rug. Water soaks into the fibers adding a darker tone. A dark-gray comforter is scrunched up at the heel of my bed.

"Where'd the comforter come from?"

Tracy doesn't respond for a minute. A part of me believes she'll tell me the truth, until she says, "Go back to sleep Aviana."

AFTER HEARING HUDSON, I start actively living. Maybe I'm hallucinating from lack of sleep but I crave to live in the delusion that Hudson is here. I hear his voice from multiple directions. My head spins on a swivel like an owl on guard. I expect to see him everywhere.

"What's wrong with you?" Tracy asks as she lowers down a grilled cheese and fresh fruit.

"Nothing is wrong with me," I answer with hungry eyes.

"You're acting stranger than usual."

"Fuck you," I say through a manic fit of laughter. I pop a champagne grape in my mouth.

"What?"

"I said fuck you, Tracy. You don't get to have an opinion. You put me in this fucking position, so as I previously said, Fuck. You."

"Feel better?"

As fast as the words drift off her tongue Tracy disappears. I have no control over myself as my eyes swath in black. I haven't been emotional or fucked up enough to sense the shift since Hudson left. I severed the connection to myself, but now I plug myself back in. My old friend is back and I start tossing and flipping every object in my room. The snap of wood feeds my frenzy. Energy pumps out of me like a noxious gas.

My spark is going to flame. We're all going to die.

No one wants to get on my level. No one wants to be on the ground. The front lines belong to me. Fine, I'll level us. I'll burn this fucker down.

Just as the hated foul blue rug smacks against the outhouse wall, I see a break in the wood floor amongst a plume of dirt. A medium-sized portion of the wood is cut out and secured back in place. I wrangle the piece of wood free to reveal a trap door. A well-greased trap door. I open it noiselessly. The panel doesn't fall back when I open it but holds sturdy at an angle wide enough for a body to fit through.

Below is a dark pit. It looks like the hole in my outhouse prior to all the toilet paper and human waste.

I jump down and fall hard on the cold earth.

Light filters through, I run to the light with all the backing of my darkness. My bare feet slap against the ground. About a quarter-mile down the tunnel the light makes a ninety-degree turn. I find an entryway that floods with light. I keel over with my hands on my knees. Breathing heavy, I swallow greedy gulps of air.

Steel bars block me from investigating more about the light's origin.

"Hello?" I pant peering between the bars without touching them. An empty cavern opens up to two hallways that aren't visible from where I'm standing.

"Hello?" I reiterate a bit rushed—a little on the panicky side —a lot on the gassed and dying side.

A shadow moves around the corner and forms itself into a tall man.

Its Hudson.

His yellow eyes make contact with my turquoise and it's like a punch. Instinctively I lunge towards the steel bars. My hands fist in a cold murderous grip—so tight, too tight, the bars are electrocuted and I surge back twenty, twenty-five, thirty feet.

My head smacks against a wall like a ceremonial gong. Air forces from my lungs. In one grand sweep, I'm there, and then I'm not.

"Wake up!" Tracy screams in my ear. She's as jarring as an ambulance siren.

"WAKE UP!" She slaps me across my face. "You idiot, I can't believe this is happening. I stop watching you for five minutes and you're running through tunnels underground."

Physical contact pulls a trigger in me. I shoot up with a quickness that even surprises myself. I toss Tracy aside, but then realize I'm finally touching Tracy. Not in the ooh-la-la way but in an I've-got-you-bitch way.

My fingers clamp down hard around her throat. I raise her to my eye level—which elevates her a good few inches, bitch is short. Her feet dangle and search for purchase.

Tracy, the little fly that buzzes out of reach is now fluttering and spazzing in my hard grip.

I shake my head back and forth tsk-tsking her for getting within arm's reach of me. "Explain yourself." I slam her against the barn door. "Tell me everything."

19

IF GLANCES COULD KILL

TRACY'S FACE turns various bright shades of red. The color rises gradually. First to her cheeks, then to her forehead where a vein pops and pulses. Sweat beads around her hairline.

With redheads, there is always curiosity if the carpet matches the drapes. I theoretically created the perfect trifecta of red—the windows match the carpet, which also matches the drapes. Tracy's a small red brick house. Compact muscle with kicking legs. Arms swinging, I watch her wear herself out. She will break first. I'll blow her fucking house down.

Gasps and spittle fly out of her mouth as she attempts to breathe and rapidly gases. My blood tracks down my arms adding a fourth shade of red from her clawing at me.

Her eyes close and she relaxes and fades in my clutches. I lower her feet to the floor. Traction and breath, I allow her a small reprieve. I loosen my hand around her neck.

"I'm twenty from Wichita..." Tracy begins, but can't finish. I slam her head back against the wall and instruct her I'm unconcerned about her, I want to fast forward to the involvement between her and Hudson and me.

Tears steam down her face.

"Hudson found me in the hills of Virginia. I wasn't responding the way I was supposed to, or so he claimed."

Tracy reddens further. She stammers about the hills having eyes. It's useless information. She might as well be giving me a dissertation about the Appalachian Trail.

Her sweat mixes and dilutes my blood. My forearms are covered in smears as though Tracy is attempting finger painting for the first time and the only colors she selected were red, watered-down red, slightly less red, and serum tinged red.

"What happened when Hudson found you?" I stress through clenched teeth.

"He took me with him."

"No shit Sherlock. Care to elaborate?"

"I was scared, and he took care of me. Told me not to worry."

"Did he seem normal?"

"What?!"

"Did you meet the Beast?"

"I was only with Hudson. I don't know what you're talking about."

"Keep talking Red."

"Hudson became obsessed with finding you. He felt pulled to Delaware. The moment he reached your town he came upon a doomsday prepper and..." She hoards air in her lungs. "I don't know what happened to the guy, but we ended up living in this barn that had a tunnel system. I bought Hudson a baby name book upon his request. He searched until he stumbled upon your name. It didn't take long, your name starts with an A. I pounded the pavement until I found you and did some investigation and undercover reconnaissance on my own. Recreating your room and bringing you here was my idea."

"You have everyone thinking I'm a liar."

"It is not my fault your friends are fickle."

"Now what?"

"I was hoping that you could help him. Hudson claims that

you ease him so he can think properly. And hopefully, he'll kill you himself." She says like she's telling me to watch out for the puddle I'm about to step in. "Hudson isn't well."

Hudson isn't well? What is the matter with him? How could he not be well? I don't recall him ever sneezing or having a cold. The man was superhuman, literally and figuratively.

I drop Tracy and she crumbles to her hands and knees.

My feet catch in the bunched-up rug. My knee smashes against the rim of the opening and I'm falling to the depths. Crashing with a bang. Searing pain encompasses my whole right side.

I limp towards the light at the end of the tunnel.

"Hudson!" I shout as I abruptly come to the electrified steel bars. He comes around the corner at a sprint.

"Are you all right?" I ask between staggered breaths. He looks around himself with confusion.

"Are you?" I yell losing my patience. His limbs seem intact, his jeans and shirt are intact. He looks the fucking same.

"Yes?" He looks discouraged. Then it sinks in. Tracy said he became obsessed with finding me. *Why would he think he lost me?* **He already found me.**

"You don't remember me?" I ask quietly.

"No."

"Why not?" I whine like an insolent child.

"I slipped and cracked my head on the kitchen table."

"You slipped on the floor?" I ask incredulously.

"Yeah, I guess there weren't any wet floor or slippery yellow placards available when Tracy was mopping the floor." He holds the back of his head as though he can still feel the pain.

"When I woke up with a concussion, I didn't remember anything. My memory is coming back slowly, but the need to find you came back like a bolt of lightning."

I stay silent and think back to my version of Hudson. How this is probably the most open he's ever been to me at one given time outside of our 'I'll show you mine if you show me yours' conversation.

He's always been the type of person that showed rather than told. If there was a song he liked, he played it loud, let it vibrate in my heels. He didn't tell me why he liked it, he just played the track.

This is a new version of Hudson. I smirk and think of the collection of Hudson versions: Terra's Hudson, Predatory/Beast Hudson, My neurotically cautious Hudson, and now Tracy's Hudson. I cock my head and take another gander at him, he looks the same. Longer hair maybe —curlier. I hate that he looks the same, I hate sharing him with someone new. *Fuck, now I have something else in common with Terra.*

The shock from my earlier fall has my adrenaline tanking like a blanket being yanked. My side pulses stronger and I curl into myself. Hoping to mitigate some pain I lean against the rock wall hard. Harder than I can control. Harder than my body appreciates.

Hudson reaches for me in attempts to catch my slumping form. I slither like a slinky going down the stairs, at first slow and then all at once.

His fingers touch the steel bars and he's shocked backward.

IF GLANCES COULD KILL, I would be dead. Curled up in a ball on the cold rock floor, I watch Tracy tend to Hudson through strands of my hair. He appears to be alive, just knocked unconscious. Maybe he'll have another concussion and wake up with a full memory.

After Tracy places a pillow beneath Hudson's head, she leaves. She doesn't say a word to me when she disappears down the right hallway. My eyes remain on Hudson like a magnet. I watch his chest rise and fall with each breath. I remember how the heart within his chest was once my lullaby. I smile and continue to watch the slow rise and fall.

———

HUDSON'S VOICE is gentle when he asks, "Do you need Tracy?"

"No," I say struggling to pull myself upright. I must have passed out while watching him breathe. I sound like a mother with a newborn, *I just can't believe he's real.* I brace myself with my right arm, but fall again as piercing pain shoots through my limb. My arm is useless, my hip is mangled, and my knee feels crushed. With a few strained heave-hos', I manage to get upright.

"Why would Tracy tell me you're not well?"

"I'm prone to blackouts," Hudson says faintly. He's sitting next to the humming bars. It's almost as if he's visiting me in prison with the partition as bars and not Plexiglas.

I nod and take his information and compartmentalize it with the stash of information I can't handle right now.

I hobble to my feet, it's only a matter of time before the sham of my usefulness is exposed. The greatest predictor of the future is the past, and I've never been that helpful in the past.

Hudson starts to say something to me but pauses and stops. He doesn't recognize me. Not like he should. Stranger, Danger. That's why I'm kept on this side of the bars. I was wrong. I'm not being utilized, I'm being used.

I take a long anguished walk back to the hole under the rug. Everyone seems to be looking towards me for answers, while all I have are compounding questions. *How much of his memory is intact? How much of his memory do I want to be intact?*

20

THE DUTIFUL ROLE

BRUTAL, the only word that can appropriately describe my current wellbeing when I wake up. A silver tray dangles just above my head. My reflection looks disgusting. I almost knock my face across the surface when it moves slightly. Or intentionally.

"Breakfast sunshine," Tracy echoes from within the confines of her attic loft. The rope does a figure eight above my face. The tray is a headache waiting to happen. An anvil without the Advil.

I pull the tray down to my lap with my left hand. Lopsided, the orange juice spills on my pancakes. I let out a grunt. "I see you're keeping your distance." One-sided operations make everything much more difficult to accomplish.

I watch my empty cup roll off and clatter onto the floor. It's plastic, they wouldn't trust me with glass. My plate and soggy pancakes are quick to follow. I'm left with a silver tray with orange juice sliding around distorting my disturbed reflection.

Two hard pebbles smack across the bridge of my nose. Two white pills.

"For the pain," Tracy says and lifts the tray back to her loft.

I search around me for the ricocheted medicine, "Thanks."

Tracy snarls, "It wasn't my idea, don't thank me."

I don't look at the pills before I pop them in my mouth. I'm either too trusting or too dumb, but either way, I hope they fuck me up. It's been too long since I've been high. Natural highs don't come my way; I always have to purchase my ride to kiss the sky.

"WAKE UP." Tracy hisses from above me as a waterfall of ice-cold water drenches my face. I wake with a scream and almost choke on the excess water that continues to pour from the ceiling. Gargling well water I bat the attack away like it's not fucking water. It is though, my moves are incredibly ineffective. All I'm producing are little pockets of air.

Instead of just continuing to swat my left hand at the water, I move my whole body and roll away from the waterfall and promptly spill off the bed. Another scream erupts from me when my right hip collides with the hard floor. My teeth snap down on my tongue. Iron weaves through my taste buds. I want to hurl.

"Hudson beckons," Tracy yells over my aching cries. A clash of emotions battle in me. *Hudson beckons? Am I to play the dutiful role as his servant? Hudson fucking beckons?* My hands tighten into fists and I push myself up.

My moods change as quickly as a season. Warmth from my cocooned nap is ruined by a fall of water. Winter blues hit me hard. Bitterness crackles through my bones. An icy bitch possesses my right side.

A soaked black nightshirt clings to my skin as I crawl and lower myself achingly down the hole that leads to Hudson's cave. This is what he wants me to do. This is what I'm doing.

I hate every step that pulls me closer to the light—to where

I'm *beckoned*. The term is acid across my tongue. Each consonant a sharp burn.

Hudson stands statuesque behind the steel bars. He tenses when he sees me limp towards him. He seems surprised by my appearance. My hair is disheveled and matted to my head.

"Just so you fucking know Hudson. Since you have clearly forgotten. I am a fucking human being and not a fucking human doing."

My thigh-length black shirt sticks to my curves. Underneath I'm naked. Normally I sleep in the buff, but being under surveillance has me wanting to put at least a layer between me and Tracy.

I lean all my weight to my left side. My shirt drips like a leaky faucet. Hudson's eyes don't leave my black shirt. "I don't know how Tracy likes to be spoken too, but I'm more than just my existence."

He opens his mouth but I continue with my diatribe, "and you can go ahead and stop looking at me like I'm on the fucking menu."

"You can't fault me for looking. All you're wearing is a wet t-shirt." His eyes aren't solely looking at me. They're devouring me.

"Well, you're lucky I even have clothes on!" *What point am I making?* My face heats in embarrassment. I cover my face with my hands hoping to wipe the shame away. All I touch is moisture.

"Do you normally not have clothes on?"

There is a long silence as I debate how to respond.

I count off reasons, "One: sleeping naked helps keep my body temperature lower so I sleep better." I point at him for emphasis. My index finger is a dagger.

"Two: it helps boosts metabolism. I'm getting my beauty rest." Pointing with two fingers makes me feel like I'm shooting peace signals at him, which is not my intended effect. Three fingers have me feeling ridiculous. It's awkward. I look down at my hand and it looks like I'm a-okaying my speech to myself.

"Three: it helps with stress. And four..." Four fingers aren't even pointing, it's directing. "... Fuck you, why am I explaining myself?!" All my fingers fist together and I punch the air. A fist is a firm resolved gesture.

"I'm not sure but I'm enjoying everything about you right now."

"Stop, you don't get to fucking enjoy me. What do you want?" I go back to single finger pointing because that's the authoritative gesture I want. I'm aggressive and angry so I jab at him.

He cocks his head to the side.

"You fucking summoned." I jab jab jab.

"No, I didn't. Similar to you, Tracy does not take kindly to being told what to do."

I use all five of my digits to direct his gaze from my collar to the hem of my shirt. "I didn't come down here wet by choice."

He smirks on wet and I want to punch him.

"Why would Tracy send me down here?"

Hudson scratches his head and he looks adorably lost for a moment. "I've been pacing."

"That explains nothing. You pace all the time."

"I do?"

I nod.

"I've been pacing by these bars hoping you would come back. I didn't call you down here. I wouldn't do that."

"Right, you're so noble. You wouldn't summon me, just abduct me."

Hudson sighs, "I didn't want to abduct you."

I punch the air as if I'm boxing a metaphorical punching bag, "I can't with you! I FUCKING CAN'T WITH YOU!"

Hudson puts his hands out with palms up. With his outstretched arms he communicates openness. Then his shoulders jerk and he's admitting weakness. "As I've made you aware, I don't remember my past."

I nod.

"Tracy and I believe that you are the key to helping me understand what is going on with me... with us."

"Us?" His fucking favorite term, *us*.

"Tracy and you included."

"There is nothing wrong with me."

Hudson puts his hands in his pockets. "My mistake, I didn't know that evolution has evolved to enable humans to act as a human match."

"It wasn't evolution."

"Clearly it wasn't."

"What do you want to cure? Don't you enjoy feeling like a superhuman?"

"Our abilities have drawbacks which need to be eliminated."

"What do you mean?"

"My blackouts aren't convenient."

"And Tracy?"

"Sunlight debilitates her."

A scream vibrates through the cave. Tracy's apparent impeccable hearing heard her secret easily lifted from Hudson's tongue.

I stand within inches of the electrified steel bars. I hear the hum, then a click and the humming ceases.

The bars are no longer electrified.

Tracy sprang the switch and left Hudson and me to demolish each other. I remember the empty threats from the old Hudson who spent weeks behind the scenes controlling himself before he even bought me a cup of coffee. Then another few weeks of casual encounters before he touched me. I honestly thought he would calm down on his security measures, but he was either in my hot embrace or struggling to fight the urge to kill me.

Now I face a Hudson who has no memory of precautions towards my safety and security. I'm completely vulnerable to his attack and I'm manic enough to want to risk it.

My hands rise. Delicately my slim fingers run along the steel bars. The caress is the kind an erotic dancer does on her pole. I'm goading for a reaction.

"Careful Aviana," Hudson says as his hand's fist at his sides. His discomfort is evident. It makes me smile.

"Scared of killing me?" I force air through my lungs. "You haven't changed. All you ever wanted is to keep me by your side, but not too close." I fist my hands in my hair and turn away from him.

"There must be a reason why I believe I need to kill you, and yet at the same time believe you are the only one..."

"I can't help you." I interrupt with my hands out, palms up like I'm showing him my cards.

"How do you know?"

"Does Hillview motel ring any bells?"

Hudson shakes his head no. He honestly doesn't remember.

"How about The Black Keys?" I ask. He looks down and paces as he always does; flipping through a mental Rolodex full of empty cards.

"Black keys? As in the black keys on a piano?"

"No, THE Black Keys," I say a bit louder. I sound like an alumnus from The Ohio State University. 'The' makes a difference.

"Saying the same thing over again doesn't help clarify. I'm not deaf. Are you talking about physical keys colored black?" We're digressing.

"No, The Black Keys are a two-man band that performs with wind chimes and musical glass."

Hudson's eyebrows crease inwards.

"You dip your finger in water and run it along the rim of a

wine glass. Different density, different resonating sounds—equal musical glass."

"Are you fucking with me?"

"No, I wouldn't think of it. The band destroys a baby grand piano at each performance. They toss out the black keys, hence the name. There's interpretive dance as well, that's how they incorporate wind chimes. It's quite magical. You introduced me to their music, and we went to a concert. We both got trashed and couldn't drive. We spent the night at the Hillview Motel."

I stop talking and stare at him, daring him to ask me for more details. Daring him to unknowingly reveal how much of his memory is intact. Lying is a skill, one in which integrating bits of the truth only strengthens the lie's foundation—allowing room for conviction. I believe my lie, does he?

Then the memory of what actually happened within the motel room assaults me; as if I'm skimming through old Polaroid photographs—I'm on my knees, both palms against a white wooden door pleading admittance. Tears streaked down my face, black lined mascara scarred the contours of my cheeks. My body trembled in desperation to help, to aid the being behind the wooden door. My hands entwined around the doorknob and I yanked in a rage. The door didn't have ears, it wasn't empathetic to my cause, it held firm.

I couldn't handle it.

Another Polaroid, I'm pushing against the door.

Another, charred handprints on the white door like I toasted or ironed the wood.

Another, I'm clawing my way through the fire created cavity. Hudson laid sprawled on the white tiled floor in a puddle of blood. The fire, my fire, flicked along the walls.

I've caused more problems than resolutions.

Again, I'm on my knees, but this time at Hudson's shoulder.

Panic crushed my lungs. One moment we were playing chess on the porch, and then the next Hudson rose to his feet shaking. He raced inside faster than I could blink. I upended an outdoor patio table in my haste to find a locked bathroom door. Chess pieces scattered. The king and queen flew in different directions.

I couldn't absorb the image of Hudson—motionless except for a subtle rise and fall of his chest. His breaths were slow and far in between. I thought Hudson was invincible.

His blood cooled. I sat and waited.

I doubled over, wrapped my arms around Hudson's body and struggled to breathe along with him.

A scream scratched its mark within my soul, it was sharp and thin like a butcher's knife. My screams sliced. My screams couldn't be differentiated between the sirens of the fire alarm. Both were wails of urgency.

I was pitiful and weak. I couldn't save the man that wanted to kill me.

He stirred.

He coughed.

Then what happened next—the quickest of snapshots—blurred motion of Hudson rolled to his side—Hudson on his feet with me thrown over his shoulder in a fireman's carry and hauled out of the Hillview motel.

The last Polaroid was of the Hillview motel engulfed in flames. Smoke billowing out the windows.

"I can't help you," I say between grinding teeth. Reliving the memories shred my heart. The feelings of utter despair and uselessness never weaken in intensity. The shock lessens, but the fear and anguish shine brighter than ever. It bubbles up from the pit of my stomach and steams out my eyes.

Hudson picks up his pacing again. He didn't expect the triggered memory to have such an impact on me.

I'm fucking bleeding emotions and he's fucking bleeding them with me.

"You should listen to The Black Keys: I'm Not the One. It's my favorite," I say and step away. My prank on deducing how gullible Hudson is lost its appeal. I've never been one for word games. I'm too direct.

"Tell me Aviana, how long were we together?"

"We were never together. We had sporadic passionate moments tainted with interruptions like your blackouts."

"What other interruptions?"

"The most recent is the surfacing of a girlfriend," I say with a vengeful smirk. I walk back up to the metal bars and grasp the steel between my fists.

"Terra ring any bells?"

21

TRIGGER

"Terra?" He says, tasting the r's.

"Yes, Terra, the Amazonian model that sleeps in your house. The very same house that I once resided in before Tracy snatched me from the woods. Terra the land, the earth, the every-fucking-thing. Terra, *fucking Terra.*"

Terra belongs to him and he belongs to her. There is no room for me. Yet here I stand. Here I'm apparently wanted. And he hasn't brought her up once. *Does he remember his first love?*

A wolfish smile makes a despicable appearance on his face.

"What happened on Halloween between the both of you?" I ask, my hands still clasped around the bars.

He rocks back on his heels, "What do you think?"

"You gave her back the necklace," I say and push off the bars and step away.

He steps closer to the bars. "Ok."

"So it's settled. The love between the both of you never faded." I take another step back.

"I wouldn't say that." Yet he doesn't ask me to come back to the bars. He lets me step away.

"What would you say?"

"I gave her the necklace."

I want to fucking hit him. Throw a rock. Feel some outward expression and release. "Let me leave. There is no purpose for me being here. I can't help you," I say and turn the corner.

"Where would you go?" His tormented voice stops me in my tracks.

I let out a spineless laugh. "If you allowed me such fortune, I would find my own way. I wouldn't stay local. Even if you aren't actively killing me, passively you keep stabbing me. Either way, I'm not living."

"If you could escape and go anywhere, where would you go?"

"Brazil... " I reply and instantly hate myself for divulging any of my vulnerabilities. "How about you?"

He pauses, "I've never thought about it."

"But you thought to ask me?"

His lip hitches up at my smart mouth. "I figured I'd always die defending my ground."

I walk away but never crawl up the hole. I wait within the shadows. I put my life on pause. I sit in the darkness—in a space that is not reality. I sit in its depths. I wallow in its blackness. I look down and I see nothing. I don't see myself. *I'm nothing.* I don't exist and I smile.

Hudson's footfalls pace the dirt floor. Back and forth he walks the boundaries of his cage.

"Who the fuck is Terra?" Hudson asks a few times before Tracy replies, "She's your ex-girlfriend." I didn't hear Tracy walk in.

"Ex-girlfriend? Aviana makes it seem..." He walks away before I can hear the tail-end.

Tracy chimes in, "It's a diamond-encrusted heart. She wears it to this day, every day." Tracy hasn't moved.

"Symbolically I returned my heart to her," he says and stops as he comes to the realization. If only he could remember Terra. It would seem likely that of all the memories to evoke, one of the girl he loved for most of his life would be prevalent to recall. But he doesn't elaborate.

Memory loss is fickle. Memories can be lost for long periods and then triggered and flood back at once. Memories are what make humans function, it's the who, what, where and the when of our lives. It's the frame in which we set our reality, edit our scenes. Capricious in nature, memories are malleable and decay and at times will vanish.

"Let me see a picture of Terra," Hudson says.

"We reconnected at the Halloween party." He adds and continues to pace and repeat himself like the sentence will help jog his memory. He must be scrolling through photos because he stops suddenly and says, "Tracy do you remember that note I had with me when I found you?"

"Yeah, all it had was my address."

"Look at the handwriting in this photo."

I'm dying to see what photo.

"Terra wrote the note," Hudson says as puzzle pieces I don't see shift into place.

BECAUSE OF TRACY'S CONDITION, there are no windows... anywhere. I used to think the lack of windows was a tool in mental warfare—sort of psychological mind-fuck. It wasn't. I'm not here for punishment. I'm only here as human valium.

After Tracy and Hudson's revelation, I find myself absent-mindedly circling the hole that leads to Hudson's cave. He hasn't asked to see me since our last encounter.

The hole is dark and still reminds me of the outhouse, I call it the shitter. Anytime I look at the hole I feel shitty. Definitely shittier the more I think about their revelation and how much I don't know the details. I want the details. I want to throw details at Hudson's face. I want to rub the grime and grit of raw salt in his wounds. I want him to feel as shitty as I do, so I jump.

I find the steel bars once again humming with electricity.

"Hello in there." I coo. Hudson saunters from around the corner with a bowl and fork in his hands.

I hate the fact that I crave him in his low-slung jeans. My mind wanders on whether our sex would be different.

I remind myself that he doesn't remember me, he doesn't remember me, he doesn't remember me.

"Tell me beautiful, what were you thinking about?" He asks.

"I'm not your beautiful. That's not my nickname."

"Tell me what's on your mind."

"Why would I do that? You never tell me what's on yours."

He folds his lips in like I'm the one being difficult, "You came down here. I'm wondering why."

"You used to call me Snow," I say trying to trigger a reaction.

"After Snow White and all her multiple personalities? Makes sense, you have quite a few."

"She didn't have multiple personalities; those were the dwarfs."

He doesn't respond. I stare at him because I'm too stubborn to say anything first.

The bars dissect his image in straight parallel lines. I wonder if there is another me living in a parallel universe on the other side of the bars with Hudson. If maybe I'm serving a kind of karmic debt and that's why I've been so mediocrely compliant and forced to live my life on this side of the bars.

"Would you like some watermelon?" He asks with a fork up and a bite-size sliver of fresh watermelon poised on the tip. My eyes light up.

"Come here." He beckons. My mind resists, but my feet ignore my better judgment.

He grimaces as he realizes the conductor he holds between his fingers. Cautiously, he meticulously threads the piece of watermelon onto my soft waiting tongue. My lips wrap around the fork and tug his hand closer until I release my bite from the silver.

"Are you still in contact with Terra?" I ask like the jealous bitch I am. Watermelon juice slips out the corner of my lips. I wipe it off with the back of my hand.

Hudson looks into his bowl of fruit like he's searching for an omen or prophecy. He comes out of the bowl's depth with another bite to drop into the pit of my mouth.

"No." He says as he skillfully retracts the fork from between the bars.

"I thought you were dating."

"I'm underground feeding you watermelon through an electric field."

My eyes hold onto his gaze; his eyes are begging me to trust. *Believe in him.*

"How did you end up here?" I ask hoping he'll expose his revelations to me.

"I met a guy at a bar."

"Classic, is this 'a guy walked into a bar' joke? Are you trying to be funny? Because that's not your strong suit."

He laughs and says, "No, I seriously met him at a bar."

"Is there a priest and a genie involved in this story?"

Hudson shakes his hand and stabs another watermelon bite for me. "No." He threads the fork. "It was during the day. Right after we ran out here."

"You guys ran out here? Literally ran?"

He takes a bite of watermelon for himself before he continues. "We backpacked and put tarps over the tent to prevent light through. We move as fast as cars. Don't you?"

"Sure, sure I do." Maybe one going twenty miles per hour, but never as fast as Hudson. My spine prickles with the thought that fairy Tracy can beat me in a foot race.

"Anyways," he says into the bowl. His eyes lift back to mine.

He knows I just gave him a white lie. "It was during the day and I couldn't sleep so I walked to the closest bar. It was just me, a doomsday prepper and the bartender. I was the new guy and the doomsday prepper was a regular. The bartender was wiping down the bar and looked relieved when I walked through the doors. I ordered a beer, and the bartender poured me a beer and gave me three shots of whiskey. Then he went to the kitchen and didn't come back."

Hudson pauses and feeds me another bite of watermelon. His attention is on my mouth and threading the fork. His mouth is open, and he reminds me of when I apply eyeliner, I can't do it without opening my mouth. Somehow my mouth being open helps me concentrate? I don't know, just as I don't know why Hudson opens his mouth to thread the fork.

"The doomsday prepper talked my ear off about the apocalypse and the walking dead. He told me about his bunker he created beneath a barn—how he purposefully kept the barn outdated without plumbing and lights. It was all a part of the facade. I appreciated the shots the bartender provided and took all three in succession. Then I grabbed the bottle and started pouring shots for me and doomsday, whose name was Henry."

Hudson slips another watermelon bite in his mouth and places the empty bowl on the floor beside him. "We were drunk by two in the afternoon. I talked him into showing me his bunker. He blindfolded me, which worked fucking horribly because it was the drunk leading the blind. Thankfully the bar was close, we only had to stumble for about a half-hour or so. Henry and I took the bottle of whiskey with us and he showed me the barn but wouldn't let me down to the bunker. I was drunk and amicable so I sat and listened to his stories for a few more hours. Eventually, I had to part ways and told him I'd visit another day. He was upset, Henry said he had some party favors if I wanted to stick around. I looked outside, and it was getting dark; I declined his offer." Hudson's lip ticks up in remembrance.

"Henry was old, and I didn't understand what he meant by party favors. It could've been anything. I was too drunk and didn't want to be manhandled in my sleep. When I found my way back to Tracy, she was livid. It was well past dark. I blacked out for the first time around her that night. Scared her pretty bad. The next day I went to the bar and Henry wasn't there. The bartender was relieved, said Henry went there every day. I walked to Henry's barn and found him naked and dead. His party favors were pain killers, and he ate a few too many and died in the outhouse."

"My outhouse?"

"Do you know of another outhouse?"

"HE DIED IN THERE? Why would you let me shit in there? Were the pills Tracy tossed at me his too?"

Hudson nods and under his breath says, "He died either taking a shit or jerking off with his hand on his dick; heart attack or overdose. Tomatoe, Tomato, right?"

Before I can stop myself, my hands grasp onto the bars and I'm sent rocketing back until the rock wall stops my fall. The words screaming off my tongue aren't the verbal lashing I wanted to give to him. I wanted to knock some sense into him and not knock the sense out of me.

* * *

I gain consciousness emerging from a buffered world as if breaking the surface of a perfect dive—or a belly flop as a ripple of pain undulates through my body. My stomach turns in knots and my head throbs. The taste on my lips is of dirty pennies, as if I used spare change for mouthwash.

My eyes lazily open. The world around me is fuzzy and twisting in dimensions.

On unfamiliar ground, though very comforting ground—

that feels similar to silk? *Am I on silk?* I can't see anything. I curl deeper into the sheets and find my curl more of a slide.

"Are you ok?" Hudson asks.

I'm ragged and torn and resemble an old stuffed animal that is no longer required for comfort. Once loved terribly and clutched tight—now I'm outgrown and re-categorized in the files for *I can't believe I did that.*

"I'm fine," I say slamming my mental filing cabinet.

"Does it still hurt badly?"

"It hurts badly," I say matching his obtuse vagueness.

The silence that follows might as well be sound waves moving through clouds of gas between stars. All my words I want to spew don't leave my lips. A heavy hum does. A sound deep as a black hole. My words are eaten up by the uniform nothing that is space. Every time I have a thought at the tip of my tongue, it disintegrates. Almost as if I'm communicating through a vacuum. I can scream and tantrum and it would be utterly useless. Essentially discarded noxious gas.

Finally, I ask an all too basic question, "Why are you treating me as a prisoner?"

He sighs, his words sucked up in the vacuum.

"Some weed wouldn't have killed you," I say and cringe at my killing reference.

"I didn't want you here. I wanted to find you and once I did, I felt relief and murderous."

"Then let me go."

"You hold memories I don't have. And I can't let you go. I need you."

"I need more dead man pills. Do you have any?"

I hear a drawer open and pills rolling around a bottle. He passes me two and I wiggle my fingers for a third. I want my being to match my words and be sucked up in a vacuum and sent off into space where I can float and stare off into galaxies. I want to be in a complex mass of vibrant colors where I can soundlessly scream.

I knock the pills back with water. Hudson holds the cup to my lips. He doesn't touch my skin and I only drink enough water to allow the pills to jaggedly make their way down my throat.

On my next exhale I release all the words into the vacuum of our space. I tell him about how I was stolen by a shadow and the ceramic tub that kept me alive. I tell him about the drugs that fueled my veins with high-octane fire. I skip our meet and greet. Instead, I move on to Hudson's life and how a car hit him and changed his direction to point to me. I gloss over the fact that I'm his hit-and-run. I don't divulge how Terra wants him back. My lips are numb when I finally mention Genevieve.

I feel each ounce of my hundred plus pounds weighing me down with gravity.

"You kicked her, and fucking kicked her, until she ran away, and I saved her. I saved her. I got to her in time." My words are sluggish and drop off my tongue. "Her in car."

"I saw you.... in window. Back of your head... But saw you and whooooooosh. Fire." I say seeing the vibrant flames behind my eyelids.

"I burn you down, I burn you down," I was breathing fire. I never felt as powerful and out of control as I did that night. I roll to my stomach and smother the sensation.

"Now you have all my memories." I say into the pillow sounding like a three-year-old trying to speak for the first time, "Nah youz haz alz me mem-row-wheez".

"Do you hurt now?" Hudson asks quietly. Almost at a whisper.

"You." Is all I say. *You.*

"You hurt me too Snow." He says, his voice touching me in places that are deep and ultimately feminine. I'm in a profound cosmic medicated stupor.

Lavender fills my nostrils. I hear a jar opening, but it might be a continent shifting. Fissures. Tea tree oil compounds with a lavender scent.

"How attached are you to this?" Hudson asks running his finger under my tank strap. There was all but one breath for me to react when he rips the strap at the seam. The second strap soon to follow. Shoulder blades bare.

Shock surrenders quickly to a tender touch that rhythmically pets the discolored marks into bliss. His hands circulate my blood and oxygenate my soul. Each press crests into a euphoric knead that rhythmically squeezes and rolls my tension away. Thumbs dig under my shoulder blades to disseminate any hard stress pockets. Each shoulder is caressed with both hands. My spine is realigned.

Warm hands lift from my body. Fingers drift off my skin.

"Wait," I say. It sounds like I said, eight or ate. "Why'd leave after fire?" My tongue fat from drugs and comfort.

"You tried to kill me. Why would I stay?"

Why would he stay? I thought I as drifted through space. Terra is an obvious choice. His friends and life would be a shady second or a tagalong addendum to the former choice.

To defend himself, another obvious choice. Being on the run only made his situation worse.

To kill me. *Why didn't he come back to kill me?* I would've come back to kill me. With all his threats and promises—why didn't he come back to kill me?

I thought I had killed him. It would have been the perfect ambush for him to come back and murder me instead.

OUT OF THE CLOSET

HUNGER PULLS me out of my sanctuary like the devil itself. Complete blackness surrounds me. Silk slips beneath my legs when I search for the edge of the bed. My hand reaches out and I touch soft velvet. Deduction places me in a high-rise coffin.

Groggy, I touch my face to make sure my eyes are open. They are. I snap my index finger and thumb together and produce the smallest spark. A microscopic pop of light to let me know that I didn't wake up blind. I do have sight.

I toss the covers off me and kick my feet off the bed. Plush carpet greets my toes. I flatten my heels into a room with walls dripping in black linen. Black velvet curtains close behind me when I stand up from the four-post bed.

I walk further into the room and caress the soft fabric of a sofa and the hard sleek surface of a coffee table. Everything is black as pitch and impeccably clean. No chalky dust residue. No powder texture for my fingers to leave prints. No knick-knacks or personal mementos.

Visually impaired I navigate my surroundings cautiously while clutching my ripped top. There's limited furniture and I find myself standing in space with no direction. I backtrack to the couch and move to the side until I touch a wall which I follow as a guiding rope.

At hip level, I find a cold handle that jiggles and rotates.

The door opens with a creak. In the silence of my movements the creak echoes and screams. I hold my breath instinctively trying to quiet the noise like my held breath could absorb sound.

A flick of a switch and a single bulb cascades light upon tousled clothing. A yellow glare is tossed upon off-white walls. I've reached a small walk-in closet and not a door out. I back up, but don't turn the light off since it's the only light in the room. I turn my back to the closet and take in the blackness of the monochromatic space. Behind me is light, white, and walls. Before me is saturated black in textures of velvet, linen, silk, shag and wood varnish.

There's a door on the opposite side of the room. Must be the exit. I turn back to the closet and reach inside to turn the light off. My fingers are on the switch when I notice the back wall isn't a solid white. There are canvases stacked facing away from the door. All I see is the soft cream of the canvas backings.

Curious, I step inside the closet and shut the door behind me. The creak is loud and groaning. Though this time, I hold my breath in anticipation. I check the handle and make sure it's shut properly and not locked. It gives a wiggle. I should have checked the door before I closed it.

I walk past haphazardly thrown clothing. Jeans and neutral shirts intermix. Silver and gold metal hangers dangle empty along the bar.

I pull a canvas closer to me and slowly spin it around. At first, all I see is an explosion of vibrancy. The color of **BOOM** assaults me.

Robbed of air I pull the next canvas, then the next, and the next. I position the canvases all around me and sit down in the center of a kaleidoscope of me coming. Eyes closed, chin tilted upward, lips parted. I'm having an orgasm in each image. The paintings are too realistic. I can almost hear myself moan. My toes curl.

They're masterpieces. Hudson made me his masterpiece. I'm stunned stupid. He remembers me. *The fucking liar remembers me.*

My hand fumbles with the door handle behind me. I stand with my back to the door and multiple versions of myself coming apart in front of me remain bold and bright. The few steps of distance do nothing to hinder their effectiveness. It's a sick carnival trip. A fucked up play on mirrors and emotions.

I push the door open and all but fall out. My eyes are wary and shine when I kick the door shut to the closet. Every shred of color wiped out instantly. A ruler of yellow light shines below the door.

My heart pounds in a mixture of fear and excitement; a wild horse of galloping beats. My breaths huff like an overrun mare, each exhale isn't fully released before the next inhale cuts it off. On my feet, I'm still but racing.

A voice slides over my body like a physical touch. "Breathe."

I stiffen and search the room. My eyes widen uselessly. I can't see—I sense Hudson in the room with me.

"Why didn't you tell me?" I ask the closet door. Hudson's body brushes against me. His shirt grazes my skin, but it might as well be a shove off a cliff.

"Tell you what? That it's been hell without you and I fear it's a worse hell to be with you. That all I remember is us fucking. Is that what you want to hear? That seeing your face is a constant reminder that you burned a house down to try to kill me. Why would I do you any favors?"

Tears burn behind my lashes. I swing like an amateur boxer. I wallop and thrash and collide with nothing but tense air.

"Well fuck you and the horse you rode in on," I pant. A tear tracks down my face and slips between my lips. "I wish you did fucking die because this," I point around me even though I can't see, "is so much fucking worse."

My breath catches in my lungs when his hand rests around the side of my throat. "I didn't do it." The heel of his palm settles along my shoulder.

I push against him, "There's no one else who fucking could have. She didn't beat her-fucking-self up."

Hudson pulls me to him, "Tracy said when I found her I was a wreck with only a note that had her address. For a while I didn't explain myself, just hunkered down with her and compared notes on our abilities." He pauses letting Tracy's story fill the empty air. Her story isn't his to tell, and the silence is suffocating.

"Eventually I told her how I loved a girl and wanted to be with her. How I bought a house and wanted to make it work. How I asked her friend to help make the surprise a real *Hallmark moment*." His fingers tighten. "I left Genevieve inside while I stepped outside to take a piss. I was in the backyard a few trees deep and figured I'd grab a bucket of water from the stream nearby in case Genevieve needed to use the restroom. I didn't go inside and tell her I had to fill the tank since the water was turned off." His thumb strokes my jugular as he relives that night. "I was walking too slow, lost in my thoughts and preparations because on my way back I heard the front door slam." His voice reverberates through my bones as I relive that night through his perspective.

"Then I moved too fast." His thumb pauses. "Someone darted out the back door. I gave pursuit deeper into the woods behind the house. They were faster than me and was weaving between trees towards the well. Once they reached the well, they disappeared. I looked all around me—I looked for too long." His other hand pulls me closer; he loosely hugs me to his chest. "When I stepped back into the house, I heard car doors slamming."

He grips me tight quickly, then he lets me go entirely and steps away.

"I made it into the living room and saw drops of blood smeared and scattered on the floor. I was looking down when I should have been looking up because the wall I was near exploded in flames."

The End. And all I could think to ask was, "You love me?"

"Apparently I *did*. When I told Tracy about that night I didn't give details or names. I didn't want to rehash the events, and I didn't want to go back. Then my concussion hit the reset button on my brain and I went running straight to the individual who betrayed me. After your drugged confessional, I think the shadow that abducted you as a child may have been the stranger that ran out of the house."

"It was a cabin, Hudson," I say and can sense his glare. My point is irrelevant because either way, I burned it down.

"What are you getting at?" I ask.

"I think it's time for us to act alive again."

"You're letting me leave?"

"I want to use us as bait," Hudson says and pulls me to him by my hips. My hands still clutch my top. I wait for his next thought, but he says nothing and neither do I.

My arms squeeze uncomfortably between us. Slowly, I wrap them around his neck. Now we're hugging and I don't think we've ever hugged before. At first, it's awkward and I start counting in my head to distract myself from wondering if I need to pull away first, or if he's waiting for me to pull away first. Maybe he's going to crush me tighter and break all my ribs and smash my internal organs and that's how I go out. That's how I die.

After ten-seconds my thoughts are spiraling and Hudson's holding a stiff board.

Twelve-seconds and he rests his head on mine and I soften.

Twenty-seconds and our breaths are matching.

Somewhere between forty-five and sixty-seconds, I lose count. I drift into ruminations about darkness and how it's a great equalizer by washing our slates clean. We're no longer Hudson and Aviana. We're male and female. We're two beings holding each other together. Obsessed with the other. Selfishly feeding off of the other's energy.

My fingers comb through his golden curls. The strands are longer; my palms pull further.

His thumbs circle at my hips.

The room gradually fills with sexual electricity. The closer we pull each other, the higher we climb up the emotional roller-coaster. Each breath is another *tick, tick, tick*—the coaster grinding up, up, up the track. Until we're at the peak and we are going to pull away filled with oxytocin or...

I rise onto my toes. His lips turn and he's kissing me, or my lips turned and I'm kissing him. It doesn't matter. *Semantics.*

The rumble in his chest—his growl, low and deep—is the only warning I have before he lifts me off my feet and takes us to bed.

The heavy black curtain shuts in a flurry of motion. I'm flat on my back with Hudson rolling his hips into me. Our lips separate and he leans back memorizing every intricate shadow and hallow that I can't see.

Hudson handles me with primal, almost feral hands.

"I feel you." His voice is thick like honey and drips into my thoughts. "I feel your desire for me." His wicked teeth leave sinful red marks. His swollen lips dictate along my collarbone, breasts, and then lower. He slips his hand along my inner thigh.

I buck into his knuckles.

"*You are mine,*" I confess in my mind and forget that he has access to my thoughts. My leggings are ripped off and I'm naked below a fully clothed Hudson.

I slip out of my mind when he slides into me.

I stay in our dark space.

I wrap my legs around him and hold him as close to me as I can.

He stays clothed and armored. He only opens his fly.

I'M LET out of my prison.

Hudson and I walk until the city lights are behind us. Hours and miles are ticked away. Each light pole is soon replaced by a tree trunk until even those become sparse.

We fade into the woods and enter into a clearing. We're on land I've scoured several times. Barren land where vegetation is resurrecting in small blades of grass.

"What is this place?" Hudson asks. He steps into the space where *the* cabin used to be and squats down to sift the dirt between his fingers, then he abruptly gets up and sprints off in the direction of the well and stream.

When he returns, I know he has the answers. The Beast in him has taken over. He surveys the area with fresh predatory eyes. This is ground zero.

"Do you remember?"

He looks at me with eyes black as night. His intense stare has me backing away, rejecting the situation. I want out of this environment. Instinctively I want to scream, *I'm not prey.*

Distracted, I didn't initially hear the voice coming through the woods and down the driveway. "2011 was the year of the Rabbit; a superficial year full of discretion." The feminine voice grows louder as it approaches. "2012 is the year of the Dragon. This is a year of power."

And as the voice moves towards us, I step further away. I drift through the trees, weaving in and out of branches watching Hudson. His eyes follow me, yet he remains rooted.

"It will work this time," says the familiar feminine tone that I recall.

But does Hudson?

"The spell Red_Nightly gave me doesn't indicate astrology or zodiac variables. But it's the year of the Dragon and a full moon, *this will work.*" The voice belongs to none other than Terra. A flashlight extends from her hand. "This is the furthest we've gone with the spell, he's *here*. We at least see him this time."

Beside her, an awestricken Genevieve brandishes her own billy club-flashlight. They both are barefoot and wearing high-visibility clothing.

"Remember, don't let him drink your blood. He won't follow or speak to us if he tastes our blood."

Genevieve cements to the ground at Terra's instructions. Her face blanches. She cringes and cowers. Her baton drops. "How could this be working?" Genevieve asks herself as she shivers like the baton's ground impact reverberated up her fixed position.

Terra continues at pace. The distance between Genevieve and Terra yawns as if on a hinge, Terra moves on a wide steady arc towards Hudson. Her feet stop a few steps away from him. Her toenails are painted bright pink. She has three silver toe-rings on her left foot. Hudson's boots are muddy and weathered. The leather is cracked and in bad need of conditioning. Genevieve's gaze won't leave his laces.

Hudson stares at Terra with a similar perplexity that a cat would during combat with a laser pointer. Could he outsmart the light? Could he ever catch it?

"You look cleaner than you should. And you're alone?" Terra asks unfurling a folded piece of paper from her back pocket. The sheet is clean and white with red scribbling. Most likely printer paper from Ben's office. Terra analyzes the words, and as she reads her lips move. Her head nods as she internally checks off her to-do list.

I'm no longer threading through the trees, I'm going deeper and further away. The image of the clearing becomes smaller, as if I'm watching them on a portable television from another room.

Genevieve whines and snivels at the bend of the driveway. Her eyes are large and frightened. Like a broken, scratched record player, she continually repeats, "How is this working? How could this be working?"

Terra circles Hudson placing long white candles around him. Her shoulder bag flattens with each candle placement.

"I don't know how much time we have," Terra says placing the fourth candle on the scorned earth.

At the last candle, a small bottle and bundle are pulled out of her bag. The bundle of herbs is sprinkled with the oil from the bottle, then lit on fire. Cedar and sage smoke puffs into the air. Terra performs a smudging ritual around the circle, around Hudson. After one full revolution, she places the smudge bundle down by the third candle. The bundle's lit end smokes into the circle. Terra then lights each candle with a white Bic.

"I'm so pleased I could find you," Terra says walking back to Hudson. Candlelight surrounds them in a kismet glow. True madness floods my system when she stops in front of his boots again. A few blades of grass slithered in between one of her toe-rings.

"Terra?" Hudson asks.

Genevieve drops to her knees at Hudson's voice. Instantly she's transported back to when she was savagely beaten at the cabin.

I don't move. I don't know what else to do but anchor myself to the tree in front of me. I press up against the bark as a spectator and not an actor.

The long-lost lovers have once again found each other.

Their history is palpable. She's *the one* for Hudson. But Hudson is no longer *just Hudson*, he's the Beast too. My pulse rises at the thought of the Beast because he craves to kill me and doesn't appear to want to harm Terra in any sense of the word.

My skin prickles in awareness a moment too late.

A coarse potato-like-sack covers my head. Sweat beads on my brow. I take rapid breaths—I'll hyperventilate before I can scream.

"Don't struggle Lily." Says a certified blast from my past. "'The Beast isn't burnt. I suffered the task of beating up that slut to enrage you, only to see he survived. Listen to me well Lily, you won't be able to enter unless you murder the Beast by your own hands. Don't give him the satisfaction of entering the Arena by your death. His next seizure will most likely be his last. If you don't kill him before he bleeds out, you will meet your demise through a coma. I want you in the Arena. You're already late. Be there before you both die. **Kill him.**"

Just as quickly as the sack slipped over my head, it disappears. My reality spins around me in a blur. Bile rises and I spew against my anchor's bark.

My feet trip over loose branches. The man from my past vanished with no traces or footfall. My shoulder slams into a tree redirecting my gaze back to the séance.

Terra stretches her arms and wraps them around Hudson's neck. Her arms are thin strands like laces that tie and secure. Her petal soft lips part and close the distance to Hudson's mouth. They kiss like first cousins.

He unwraps her arms and pulls away from her like he's trying to get out of a cobweb. She smiles feeling their connection —not quite grasping the vibe.

"What happened the last time we spoke, during Halloween?" Hudson asks scanning around the séance circle. It's almost as if he's on stage, he can't get past the glare and see the audience. Genevieve is a shadow. My presence may only be sensed.

"How did Red_Nightly know you'd ask that?" Terra refers back to her white sheet of paper with black scribbles. Her lips move again as she reads. This time faster, presumably since she is skimming. She flips the page over, it's blank.

Collapsing her note along the over-folded creases she says, "You gave me back my necklace and we started fighting. You didn't want to cause a scene, so you asked to take me back to my hotel, where we fought more until you fell asleep on the couch during a stalemate."

"What were we fighting about?"

Terra lets out a frustrated sigh, "What weren't we fighting about is a better question. You bought a cabin that you didn't want to show me. You told me you forgave me, and you loved me, but you weren't in love with me in the same way that you used to be. You didn't want to be with me the way I wanted to be with you. The constant theme was that you changed and you couldn't trust yourself to be real with me. Your life was complicated and somehow intertwined with Aviana."

Terra takes a deep breath and then adds the puncher. "You're standing on the cabin's ruins. And Aviana isn't returning, she's gone. She ran away a while ago. Hudson, let me take you home. I'll take care of you the way I should have. I'm not scared anymore. I can help you figure out what's going on. I love you, let me take you home."

Genevieve crawls and fumbles to her feet in mixed hysterics back towards the main road.

"You should take care of your friend," Hudson says.

Terra turns as if it just dawned on her that Genevieve came with her. Within the split second that Terra's eyes left Hudson, he slips into the shadowed woods away from her sight. A car door slams shut.

23

RAT-TAT-TAT

ALL OVER AGAIN, in a sick and twisted déjà vu, I feel my life slip between my fingers like sand grains in an hourglass.

Can my own breath strangle me?

I know not thinking is just as easy as keeping my eyes open when I sneeze, or not sneezing when I stare at the sun.

Is it voluntary or involuntary?

How much actual control do I have over my life?

Am I even living?

Crouching beside a flowing stream, I hold a stout reddish-purple stem. There are fifteen tiny white flowers clustered together in an umbrella shape. I spin the plant in a full revolution like a ballerina in a jewelry box. I hum a soft tune imagining I'm a baby grand.

Snap. Crunch.

Twigs and debris break and shift under a weight heavier than squirrels and woodland creatures.

"I wasn't expecting you," I say rubbing the whitish film from the ripped stem, "at least not so soon." I rinse my fingertips of the oily sap.

227

"It's not like that Av," Hudson says from behind me. "It's time for us to leave." He steps closer. "We've spent too much time here and need to keep looking-"

"Don't lie to save my feelings. It is like that. It will always be *like that*." I count each small petal to each small flower.

"Who's Red_Nightly?" I ask assuming it's Tracy, yet I need to hear him confirm. My brain is working a hundred-piece puzzle and I've only found two corners and five side pieces. Hudson's confirmation will only be an ambiguous, all one color piece that fits centrally. Yet I need that extraneous piece for the full picture. I need him to say it.

"We don't have time for this."

"Fuck, it is *her*, isn't it? She sent Terra and Genevieve out here to find you." I mentally slam my fists against the table holding my hundred-piece puzzle conundrum. Small jigsaw pieces' scatter like thieves in the night. "He found me. Did Tracy send him too?"

Breath sucks out of his two lungs. "You saw him?"

I dry my cold wet fingers along my jeans. The wet lines are dark stripes. "What if I told you that your next blackout will be your last—I might be able to save you—but I don't know what will happen to you." I add water from the stream to the thermos' cup. The thermos is empty now, but the cup is still useful for a drag.

"You're rambling Aviana."

"I know... I know... I can't watch you die again—I know you didn't die before, but it felt like you died. The point is, I might save you from dying. I'm willing to take the risk. I mean, I *want* to take the risk. And I'm *not* fucking going back to that fucking barn."

Hudson addresses me like a psychiatric patient about to be committed. He speaks in the most normalizing manner—sticking to facts and not using any highly stigmatized words.

"What's going on Av? You saw the man? Start from the beginning."

"No, I didn't see him." Technically, I didn't.

"You said he found you. Then I find you pulling weeds."

"I know," I say on a puff of breath and wipe my arm across my brow. "I know, ok, here, can you hold this for a second?"

He concedes and pulls the plant from my grasp—the *Cicuta maculata* is in his left hand. He clutches the stem like a home-coming date handles a boutonniere—as if it will likely stab him. I hand him the half-filled thermos cap to hold in his right hand.

Rising to my feet, I'm literally and figuratively exasperated of not being able to see the forest—I'm overwhelmed and claustrophobic by the individual trees.

"This is the only way I can explain." Quickly, like livestock grazing, I wrap my mouth around the umbrella flower. I gag on petals. I pull, fold, and try to swallow as much plant particles as I can. I manipulate the flower like it is three strands of Twizzlers that are eaten at once. I chew the stem and spit out the very end. I wave my hands around requesting the cup of water without actively asking.

Hudson grabs the back of my head and tips the cup to my lips. The flavor is foul before turning out-right bitter. My mouth is filled with a slurry that is chunky and tastes nothing like herbs. Nothing like wild carrot should.

The thermos cup is discarded. It plops into the stream and is taken away. I swallow multiple times until I'm only swallowing big gulps of air. The taste and texture don't leave. The flavor is shellacked thick on my tongue.

ACID BURNS and crawls up my throat like a climber performing a free solo ascent of my laryngopharynx, to my oropharynx, then wrapping around my palatine tonsil. I wipe the back of my hand across my mouth and spit bile onto the rolling earth.

The ground moves like the undulations of snake movement. The surface laterally bends. *If I stop moving would I be propelled forward?*

"Are you sure that was a wild carrot?" Hudson asks for the umpteenth time. My actions are not fitting any algorithm. He doesn't understand my explanation that movement is happening too fast. Life is too random and unexpected to process facts. Everything is too fucking fast.

Hudson is still talking, but I zoned out after his question. I can't process information at the same rate he does.

We're holding a different set of cards.

Surrounding trees pick up their rooted feet and march alongside us. Hudson doesn't notice. I smile. My lips slip against my teeth which feel like porcelain tiled gates.

"Of course, it was water parsnip," I say. Smoke laces my words. I whistle a stream of smoke rings. A chain-smoking dragon lives within me.

Hudson stops.

The trees and I continue to walk. Their limbs lean closer, the leaves rustle like a beaded curtain. The leaves are neither transparent nor translucent, they're frosted glass cut in the shape of leaves. A pearl sheen pollen rubs off on my fingertips; the texture is velvety. I expected the leaf to be crisp like paper— the thinness gives the illusion the leaves are brittle and fragile.

"You've seen me with horticulture books before. These are things I know. Book things are my things." I rub my fingers across the surface and it changes colors, similar to ther- mochromic pigments, with each swipe of my thumb a new color is revealed. It reminds me of the horse from the Wizard of Oz that continually changes colors. That horse is my favorite character from the Wizard of Oz and we only see a glimpse of the majestic animal.

Distracted, I trip and fall to my knees in a wet spot. My pants soak up the ground's muck. A scuttling noise catches my attention. I jump to my feet expecting a raccoon or possum. I turn to see Genevieve crawling out from a culvert dripping in sludge with tears streaking down her face. Mascara rims her eyes. She has the same hysterical gleam that she did the night I picked her up out of the woods when she was beaten. *These fucking woods.*

Genevieve's limbs snap in directions that aren't anatomically permissible. Her legs acquire the genu recurvatum deformity, they hyperextend and bend backward. Her back bends into a spider walk made famous from *The Exorcist*. With her head tipped, she cackles, then screams, "Run!!"

My feet kick off and slide back as if on a treadmill. Momentum flings my body forward and face-plants me deep in filth. I push off the forest floor and run directly into Hudson. The slurry transfers to his shirt. The mark is a perfect replica of my face. I lift the bottom of my shirt and wipe the rest of the muck out of my eyes. Hudson, Genevieve, and the trees see a flash of the underside of my breasts.

I drop my shirt and open my eyes to clear vision. Hudson is still in front of me. Obscenities drip off his tongue. The trees are back in their rooted position. There is space. The forest has righted itself.

Hudson snaps in front of my third eye. I focus on his fingers. But I can't for longer than a few seconds. There's movement behind him, Genevieve, she's outnumbered by her hallucinations. She sweeps her legs, kicks, punches, and spins around trees and invisible offenders. A horror of a dance of war that Hudson is oblivious to.

"You're burning up," he says with both hands on my cheeks —I can't feel them—I can't feel anything but heat.

I'm dying and it's liberating. There are no rules. There are no more risks. There is only *right now*.

The leaves on the tree behind Genevieve's dance of war shake like maracas. A skeletal Terra slides down a tree's limb in a white dress composed of multiple, sheer, glittery layers. Just as she appears, she disappears.

"Your pupils are huge." Hudson's grip tightens on my jaw. He holds my head closer to his. In my peripheral Terra reappears, she's still skeletal, but now her face is painted for the Day of the Dead. She moves like a ballerina on the tips of her toes towards us.

Horrified, I spin and see a broad, flat, horizon. I see where the sun sets. The purest cornflower blue sky has floating cotton candy pink clouds, thin strands of spun sugar high in the sky. Plum streaks of altocumulus layers create the seam between cornflower blue and the signature fiery orange of a sunset. Hot-pink slashes the underbelly of the plum and across the orange like a searing knife bleeding the heavens. Yellow relaxes and fades beneath the angry, vivid hues. The sun is setting.

I'm running.

I'm in a mad dash. Each of my arms are spread out, I'm fucking flying and am impervious to danger. I'm a Lockheed Martin F-35 Lightning II combat aircraft, I can fire up to 3,300 shots per minute, and I'm about to **rat-tat-tat** every-fucking-thing. I'm a free bird.

EPILOGUE

HUDSON

SHE'S NOT LISTENING. I'm screaming her name and she's not listening.

I give chase and tackle her before she can run further away from me. We tumble, skid and scrape—I take the brunt of the road rash. Gravel tenderizes my forearms like a meat grinder.

Aviana's heart is pumping too fast. A sheen of sweat covers her skin. Hot blood smears and pools around us. She begins to shake and convulse. Her mouth opens; she's trying to tell me something but her throat is closed shut. Sputtering bubbles pop off her lips. I grip her jaw and tilt her head back to keep her airway open.

I can't let her go. With broken vocal cords I plead, I can't let her go.

She's burning too hot for my touch.

Her eyes roll back.

I lay her onto her side. My hands cushion her head. Sweat pours rivets down my face. I can't let her go.

A burning light explodes out of Aviana and I'm thrust away.

My head smacks and cracks against a rock rushing blood down my face and neck; another geyser on my body. My vision blurs and skews to see Aviana smoke and continue to convulse. Crawling against fractured ground, I wrap my body around her and catch fire.

We're both ablaze.

And they say legends never die.

ACKNOWLEDGMENTS

Evansville Drive wouldn't be Evansville without my dear friend Chinchs. Thank you Sarah.

I'm grateful for the early acceptance and support from Ashley & Mary Frame—who is sunshine.

Thank you Rainbow Unicorn, you are the bestest Gallo. My unfiltered sarcasm sees you—you help me back to a peaceful path.

My husband holds the kite. He's my best friend. I love our life.

My sincere gratitude to the ladies who read drafts, beta versions, and random sentences. Thank you for encouraging me to share my art. And thank you for showing up.

I appreciate the reader, whoever made it to this sentence here. I truly thank You.

ABOUT THE AUTHOR

C.B. Wiant lives in Ohio with her husband and dogs. She graduated with a Bachelor's of Science in Biology from The Ohio State University. She considers herself an artist—and is truly grateful she is able to share her art.

Connect with C.B. Wiant on Instagram: @CBWiant
     She's interested in your perspective and will most likely profusely thank you for reading her words.

LIT

Welcome to the Arena.

Made in United States
Orlando, FL
15 December 2021

11709305R20152